More Dam Trouble

Earl H. Smith

North
Country
Press

More Dam Trouble

Copyright © 2014 by Earl H. Smith

Cover art by Kathy Speight Kraynak.

Library of Congress Control Number 2014932188
ISBN 978-0-945980-77-3

This book is entirely fiction. Period.

For Kelly, Jeff, and Mike

Acknowledgments

Let's be clear about a couple of things, right off the bat. First, although this book will very likely be called a sequel, I assure you that it can perfectly well stand up on its own three-plotted feet. If you happen to be among the millions who have yet to read *The Dam Committee* (North Country Press, 2011), you won't feel at all left out if you choose to read this one first.

Also, I'm afraid I need to say that there is no place called Belfry anywhere in Maine. Even so, we all know small towns very much like it, where the natives enjoy embroiling themselves in every controversy, large or small, and where events as startling as a murder can positively turn things upside down. It follows, of course, that the people in this book are made up as well, cobbled together from bits and pieces of the kinds of intriguing characters found in most every small town in America. While I'm sure some readers will get a kick out of making ties between these fictional characters and the real people they know, I assure you that the exercise is one of sheer folly.

While I have this space, there are, in fact, some very real people I want to acknowledge. Foremost among them is Patricia Newell, the gracious and talented publisher at North Country Press. Without her confidence and assistance there might not have been any book at all. I am also grateful to a number of folks who supplied ideas, expertise, and advice along the way: attorney Wally Buschmann, criminal pathologist John Chowning, retired state trooper Michial Heino, and several local raconteurs including Judy Johnson, Jim Meehan, Diane Oliver, Reggie Perry, Bill Pulsifer, Jack Schultz, and others who may not even realize that they helped. I am also deeply indebted to three good friends and picky readers. Without the close scrutiny of Charles Ferguson, Ron Smith and Fred Letourneau, the text might easily have been riddled with distracting and annoying errors.

Thanks as well to my children, to whom this book is dedicated, and to my wife Barbara and my Golden Retriever Benjamin, all faithful supporters of me and connoisseurs of life in a small town.

Earl Smith
Belgrade Lakes, Maine
2014

Table of Contents

1

Grand Ending

As usual, the Maine spring had come and gone at least a half-dozen times in March, and the weary folks of Belfry Village were made to keep both snow blowers and lawn mowers at the ready while they waited for things to sort themselves out. By the time the miserable month had come to an end, the locals were starving for any sign of promise, and at Knight's General Store, where the weather was the crux of almost every conversation, reports of a single, shivering robin or a doubtful daffodil or two were enough to set off wild rounds of cheerful hooting and a great deal of backslapping.

Harry wasn't at all taken in by the growing optimism, nor did he endear himself to anyone when he insisted there would be another snowstorm or two, or pointed out the large rafts of rotting ice still lumbering on the nearby lakes. Nibber, on the other hand, preferred to see the brighter side of things, and this afternoon, as he wrestled his tired Chevy pickup slowly along Shore Road, he did his best to elevate Harry's sour mood. "See there," he exclaimed, nodding at a crop of pussy willows, finally sprouting leaves. "And there," he said again, pointing out a scattering of yellow coltsfoot, aping dandelions along the ditch.

Harry was unmoved. Instead, he clung even more desperately to the exposed springs of the passenger seat and pleaded with Nibber to slow down as the truck clunked in and out of potholes the size of laundry baskets.

It didn't help that Harry hadn't wanted to make the trip in the first place. He'd made his case for staying at home when Nibber came by the Crockett house after lunch and announced they simply had to ride into the village and check things out at the dam. Harry called it a bad idea at once. First of all, it was Saturday, a welcomed day of rest from his work at the sawmill. Less selfish than that, Diane was about to have the baby, and it didn't seem proper to leave her home alone.

Before the first excuse was even out of his mouth, Harry knew it was a waste of time with a man who had no regular employment, but he was surprised when Nibber scoffed at the notion of keeping an eye on Diane. Over the last several weeks, without any encouragement at all, his friend had begun to view himself as a third expectant parent and was making a pest of himself in the process.

Still, Nibber insisted on making the trip. Not only was it the first day of April, but also the weather was clear and warm. The combination guaranteed that swarms of fishermen would be milling around the dam, paying no heed whatever to the warning signs and jostling each other dangerously for casting spaces along the spillway. Worse than that, if the past was any lesson, an idiot or two had surely crept out onto the slick and dangerous moss on the granite at the top of the dam wall. Yes indeed, as members of the Belfry Dam Committee, it was their sure and sworn duty to check things out. Harry surrendered when he realized they could drive up to the dam and back in the time it would take to change Nibber's mind.

The road along Herman Point narrowed as it wound through a stretch of old pine, and Nibber took his hands off the wheel to let the Chevy steer itself through the deep ruts. Harry's dog Winston, cramped in the middle with his long legs straddling the shifting lever, wasn't happy with the bumpy ride, either. Harry tried holding his arm in front of the dog's chest to keep him from sliding off the seat, but the retriever was dismissive, shoving Harry's hand away with his snout. With that settled, the two bounced along in perfect, sullen harmony.

"Frankly, I don't know why anybody bothers to fish today, anyway," Harry blurted out as the truck lurched around a corner. "Too early. Too cold. No hatches. No salmon. That simple." Harry knew from the buzz at the post office that a number of locals had been skulking around the open edges of the lakes for weeks, hoping for an early catch while doing their best to evade the local warden, Hannah Dimble, who up to now had bagged more poachers than the poachers had bagged fish.

"It's not called April Fool's Day for nothin'," Nibber said, reaching cautiously for the shifter, trying not to irritate the crabby dog. "Anyway, if a body had to actually catch fish in order to enjoy fishing, nobody would bother to go fishing at all."

Nibber's axioms often gave Harry pause, and he simply straightened his coat and gazed solemnly out the window. Nobody spoke until they rounded the last turn toward the center of town. "You know somethin'?" Harry piped up in rhetorical fashion. "The Village of Belfry is fast headed for hell in a hand basket."

"Say wot?" Nibber squirreled up his face and swiped his nose with the hem of his tattered Dam Committee T-shirt.

"You know what I'm talking about," Harry said. "It started last year, when Doc O'Neil got himself popped off right here in Belfry. A murder in these parts is rare enough, but it turns out this guy was a real-life hood, the Boss of the Black Wharf Gang, no less. Just imagine, a rotten Massachusetts drug dealer, shot square through the head, right here under our very noses."

"Oh, but that's all past history now." Nibber was matter-of-fact. "Besides, we got the mess sorted out in jig time."

"You mean *I* got it sorted out," Harry corrected, "and don't forget, we've still got the tricky business of dealing with the rest of the money Doc left behind." The thought made him stiffen. "We never should have taken it. Godamighty, Nibber, you know we were damn lucky we never got caught."

Nibber's blue eyes twinkled as he leaned out beyond Winston's long nose. "Still plenty of time for that," he chuckled.

Harry didn't think he was funny. "Anyway," he said, "I'm not talking about the murder, or the money for that matter. When I say this place is doomed, I'm talking about *that*!" He jabbed his thumb out Nibber's window. The sun had dissolved all but a few last stubborn patches of snow, and it was plain enough to see what had once been a broad, sweeping lawn, now long unkempt and overgrown with puckerbrush and saplings. At the very top, on a perch overlooking Finger Lake, were the blackened ruins of The Belfry Grand Hotel.

Nibber pulled off to the side and wound down his window. Winston stretched over his lap for a better view, and all three gaped up the wide slope. All that remained of the old resort was a long, low mound of ashes, interrupted here and there by charred timbers, bowing over the rubble like black-robed mourners. The dismal sight reminded Harry of photographs he had seen of wartime bombings, and he shook his head. "It's a real shame we never got to see The Grand when it was booming," he said. "Gus Gammon says it was quite the mecca."

His boss at the sawmill liked telling of long ago summers when city folks came by the trainload, filling The Grand's hundred rooms and spilling over into smaller inns and boarding houses along the narrow Main Street. Nibber nodded. Like many locals, the Nabroski family had strong ties to the old place. His father had been a groundskeeper at the hotel, long before Nikolai was born.

Once again, Harry went over the sorry tale in his head. Soon after World War II, when the automobile opened a broader menu for summer escapes, passenger trains stopped coming, and The Grand was closed and shuttered. In the years that followed, the elegant old resort slowly slid into a state of polite decay.

"Gotta admit," Nibber said, interrupting Harry's reverie, "for a while there last fall, things were lookin' up."

"Yeah, well," Harry muttered, "if we hadn't been so wrapped up in other matters, we'd have figured out exactly what that snot Ned Rafferty was up to the minute he set foot in town." Rafferty, Belfry folks were late to discover, was the stalking horse for a Boston syndicate that had quietly bought The Grand from the long-suffering and non-tax-paying descendants of the original owner. First word of the purchase came when town manager Susan Hanson received the notice of sale and mentioned it to the librarian and chief town gossip, Mal Grandbush, who that very day sashayed up and down Main Street like the town crier, proclaiming Belfry's second coming.

Like all newcomers, Rafferty should have been the subject of intense local scrutiny, but instead he slid in under the radar, on the heels of Hurricane Clara, when local gossip was firmly fixed on high water and winds, murder, and money. He rented a cabin near the dam on the property of the local realtor, Jeff Molony, and the two instantly became fast friends. Nobody paid much attention until Rafferty began to cozy up with town officials and hang out with the regulars at the Sunrise Grill, doing his best to convince anybody who'd listen that he was the new messiah, bringing salvation to all of Belfry. For a time, even Harry was taken in.

Now, as they gawked at the ruins, Harry remembered the afternoon last November when Nibber stormed through the door of the Crockett house and proudly announced he'd been taken on as a jack-of-all-trades on the renovation crew at The Grand. It was truly astonishing news. For the first time in his life, Nibber was on a regular payroll, and he made Harry and Diane follow him outside where he proudly displayed the freshly swept bed of his decrepit Chevy. A summer's worth of accumulated trash had somehow disappeared, and assorted tools were all cleaned, oiled, and lined up, ready for work.

"I'm a gopher, really," Nibber admitted. "But I'll bet I can work it into a permanent position when the place finally opens." Harry was delighted – and relieved. It wasn't hard to help Nibber find odd jobs with the flatlanders for the eight or ten weeks of summer, but turning up paying customers for the remaining three or four seasons was nearly impossible.

As they pulled back onto the main road, Harry was sure Nibber was mulling over the same sad ending in his head. Nibber had been at work barely three weeks when, on a freezing, windy night in late December, The Belfry Grand went up in flames. The volunteer fire department worked desperately to save it, but it took a half-hour or more to run hoses down to Finger Lake and another fifteen minutes to chop holes in the ice. By the time they were ready to fight, the wind-swept blaze engulfed almost all of the wood shingled building, and the giant turret on the north end became a gigantic Roman candle. Within an hour, the long veranda that ran the full front of the building collapsed backwards into the pit of flames, and the entire three-story structure was down to the ground.

Early on, word in the village was that the blaze was caused by callous renovation workers, and a few, especially Molony, put an accusing finger firmly on Nibber, who had been pulling new wiring on the day of the fire. Never mind that the power wasn't yet connected, Molony seized any opportunity to challenge the competence of members of the Dam Committee, whom he freely labeled as fools. As something of a male chauvinist, Molony generally left Nibber's girlfriend Debbie out of the mix, but Harry had seen his wrath nearly every time the Committee tinkered with the level of the lakes. Of the three committee members, Nibber was far and away his favorite target.

The realtor's contrived theory on the fire came into full public view the following week on Karaoke Night at the Sunrise, where Nibber had gone to pick up Debbie at the end of her waitress shift. Molony was on the singing stool, aping Jose Feliciano and singing *Light My Fire*, when he began to toy with the lyrics. At the first repeat of "Come on Nibber, light my fire," the accused launched out of the booth where he was waiting and plowed Molony off his perch.

The two rolled on the grease-stained carpet for a time, cussing and flailing away while the karaoke microphone, snagged in the twisting bodies, amplified the noise to the great delight of the good old boys lining the stools along the bar. Deputy Sheriff Kelly Hallowell, off duty and minding her own business in the back, was slow to respond. Finally, when Nibber reached for a catsup bottle, she waddled up front and stuck her nightstick in his ribs just as he was about to squeeze a dollop into Molony's ear.

The scuffle ended as quickly as it had begun, but Nibber steamed for three days until the state Fire Marshal's office issued its report saying the blaze was of "undetermined origin." Whether it specifically vindicated the workmen or not, there was no mention of electrical causes, and Nibber was off the hook.

Except for Molony, nobody in the village ever believed the renovation crew had a thing to do with the blaze. Instead, most of the locals expected – many even hoped – that the probe would turn up evidence of arson and point to Ned Rafferty. But instead, the report said only that the fire began on the newly oiled wooden floor of The Grand's main floor dining room and then spread up the walls and into the guest rooms on the floors above. Although the word "arson" was not mentioned, Rafferty knew what most people thought, and he took pains to explain from one end of town to the other that he and his buddy Molony were both out of town the night of the fire. The two alibis gained credibility when, one night after a few beers at the Sunrise, Deputy Kelly let on that police investigators were satisfied that the men were in Boston at the time, meeting with the investors for the new Grand. There were witnesses, she said, who swore it was true.

Even so, local suspicions only multiplied the week after the report was issued, when Rafferty marched into the Belfry Town Office and filed application on behalf of a new enterprise named Pond Park, for a giant theme park to be built on the grounds of the old Belfry Grand. The insurance company had paid up, and Rafferty and his cohorts were headed in new directions.

News of Pond Park set off an explosion in the village. While last year's mysteries of the murder and the missing money had split the town a dozen different ways, the notion of having a circus in their midst divided the place smack down the middle. On one side were those who dreamed of jobs and lower taxes, and on the other were those who feared Belfry would become the Old Orchard Beach of Central Maine. Nearly everybody was either decidedly for or dead set against the idea, and firm lines were soon drawn throughout the village. Knight's Store suddenly developed two rows of grim customers at the cash, opposing neighbors barely grunted to each other at the post office, and booths at the Sunrise became segregated by Pond Park position. The only person who seemed to be on the fence was the Rev. Eugene Peppard, pastor of Falling Waters Church, who worked tirelessly to calm his splintered flock.

From the beginning, Harry had been on the side of the mortifieds. At first, Nibber was somewhat taken by the idea of having miniature golf so close at hand, but Harry soon shamed him out of the whole idea.

Now, as Nibber wheeled past the Sunrise Grill, they could see the parking lot was beginning to fill up with assorted beaters and pick-ups. Nibber predicted a good tip night for Debbie, which prompted Harry to observe that it was fortunate one of them had a job, and he was about to make yet another plug for the institution of marriage when he thought better of it. Instead, he simply groaned. "The trouble with people around here," he said, not so subtly, "is that they tend to put things off until it's too late." For emphasis, he pointed off to the left where a worn and faded **FOR SALE** sign on the front lawn of Fritz Grunwald's place had been freshly propped up on its stake, and a new red-lettered strip, **SALE PENDING**, was pasted over the front.

"Now, there's proof," he said. "You can bet that sale is going to Rafferty's crowd. It's the last piece of the puzzle before the final permit is issued for Pond Park. Only a matter of days, I suspect. Then the jig is up."

"Maybe not," Nibber came back. "They need the Grunwald place in order to have room for off-road parking for the theme park, but there's more to it than that. Rafferty's bunch won't complete that sale until the environmental protection people sign off on the entire project, and that won't happen until they have the final public hearing next Tuesday."

"A mere formality," Harry huffed. "The only reason they're having a second hearing is because they want to be able to say at the end that they gave the opponents a fair shake. Trust me. It's all over but the shouting – and there's sure gonna be lots of that."

Nibber slowed the truck when they reached the beginning of the narrow Main Street leading up to the dam, and Harry settled more comfortably in his seat and looked out the window. Well-kept cape homes and converted inns were lined cheek-by-jowl on both sides of the road, their fronts a scant few feet from the sidewalk and their backsides facing sloping lawns leading down to Mosher Stream and Grand Pond on the right and Finger Lake on the left. The streamside Belfry Inn was still shuttered, but would be open for Mother's Day, when Chuck and Suzette Greaver returned from the islands. The tiny boutique shops were already showing signs of sprucing up. Windows were cleaned of the winter splatter of snowplows, and porches had sprouted new displays of arts, crafts, and antiques.

It struck Harry that the quaint charm of Belfry was best displayed right here, at the village center, where summer tourists would soon be disturbing the peace and spending lots of money. Most of them would say they came for the quaintness, and the peace and quiet. What would they think when the place suddenly sprouted a theme park and tourists of a very different sort? "We're doomed," he said to Winston, having wasted the line on Nibber. "This place is about to explode, no matter how Tuesday's hearing turns out."

Harry was about to go on when he glanced up the road and promptly bolted upright in his seat and pointed straight ahead, out the window. "Be damned," he said with a hint of satisfaction in his voice. "There's big trouble up ahead!"

2

Battle of the Bridge

Vehicles were backed up three or four deep on both sides of the dam, their bleating horns ignored by a crowd gathered up smack-dab in the middle of the bridge. Nibber wheeled into the last open spot in front of the post office, and Harry opened his door before they even stopped. Winston vaulted over his lap to lead the way across the street where John Knight was leaning on his gas pumps, gawking at the commotion while keeping an eye on his empty store.

"What in hell is going on?" Harry gasped when he and Nibber caught up with the dog, already on his back, legs splayed, letting John scratch his belly.

The storekeeper gestured up the road. "I'd say we're havin' ourselves a referendum."

"A referendum? On what?"

"Belfry Pond Park, that's what."

The notion made Nibber chuckle. "And, how's all that coming out?"

"As you can see," John replied with a smirk, "They're still in the discussion stage, not quite ready to vote."

Harry nudged Winston gently with his toe, and the three headed up toward the dam, where it was easy to tell that all of Nibber's fussing about the safety of fishermen had been a total waste. Nobody was fishing. Nobody was on top of the dam. Nobody was even anywhere near the water, although in the spillway at the edge of Finger Lake there were a number of small boats nudged onto the shore, their painter lines loosely lashed to the low-growing alders. The anglers had apparently joined the fray or, Harry thought, maybe even started it.

Close up, they could see there were actually *two* noisy crowds, one facing the other, formed up like flying geese, splayed out in wide V's behind their leaders. Several members of both teams were in waders, dripping water; some brandished fishing rods. One or two were waving nets. Everybody seemed to be yelling at once, and the wailing reminded Harry of the annual Loon Calling Contest, held on this very spot on the Fourth of July. But now, instead of mournful cries, the air was filled with rants and cusses, punctuated now and then by a somewhat startling "f" bomb.

Harry recognized the front goose, facing them. Horatio Perkins was wearing rubber hip boots, legs spread wide of necessity. A frayed tan bucket hat was scrunched on his head, and he waggled an old wooden oar over his head, its rowlock still attached and clanking. Harry wasn't surprised to see Horatio up front. Although everybody knew he was a gentle soul, of late he had become one of the lead opponents of Pond Park. Moreover, because he was nearly deaf and was forced to shout even to hear himself, he was, without any doubt at all, the loudest.

A few feet away and facing up the road, Horatio's counterpart general, Jeff Molony, was leading the pro-playground revolutionaries. Nibber nudged Harry, used his favorite nickname. "Who else but Bolony?"

"Of course," Harry said. "The same guy who's bent on selling every last acre of Belfry back to Massachusetts."

Molony's sweaty bald head glistened in the afternoon light, and his face was an unhealthy shade of crimson. The short, stout man was just then screaming a string of creative epithets directly at Horatio, who, it occurred to Harry, probably would not have known what the words meant even if he could make them out.

Molony's wingman was Pond Park's lead developer, Ned Rafferty, clearly running the proponent's case from the second row. Seeing the pair together made Harry bristle. Molony could never survive without a sidekick telling him what to do. His crony had once been Fred "The Deacon" Jalbert, but Jalbert had moved downstate and wasn't coming back. The abandonment coincided almost perfectly with the exit of Molony's wife, who disappeared as well, taking the children with her. The realtor had rattled around in his big house at the foot of the spillway for a month or so and was ripe for an accomplice when Rafferty arrived in town. The pair quickly teamed up on the Pond Park project with Rafferty in charge and Molony doing his dirty work. Nibber said it was a match made in hell.

Harry watched as Molony stepped off the front line and moved back to consult with Rafferty, who tilted his head back, made the reading glasses on his forehead aim skyward, and peered haughtily down his pig-like nose. From a distance, it looked as if Molony might be taking directions directly from the man's flaring nostrils.

Nibber leaned to mutter in Harry's ear and pointed at Rafferty. "Isn't there just somethin' about that man's face that makes you want to smack it?" Harry grinned for the first time all day.

Strung out behind the ringleaders were the rest of the playground supporters, and it suddenly struck Harry that many were local officials and business people. Town Manager Susan Hanson was standing with road commissioner Bo Chilton, and strung down the wing were Kerri Woods, owner of Lake Lodge; Debbie's boss at the Sunrise, Emily Boulette; and the postmaster, Hummer Humbolt. At first, Hummer seemed out of place, but then Harry remembered that for years the Belfry Post Office had been on every federal list of possible closings, prompting Hummer to wage a vigorous campaign to rent boxes and preserve the Belfry zip code. Having Pond Park would certainly help the cause.

The crowd that branched out behind the oar-waving Perkins held few surprises. Most were regularly at the forefront of efforts to foil any new local development. To date, they had been quite successful. They had managed to stall plans for a second blinker light in town and, although they lost, they had put up a good fight to keep from widening the sidewalk on Main Street.

The only newcomer in the "leave it alone" crowd was Gabe Brumbley, who had sold a parcel of land to Molony in February before realizing it was to become part of the new park. Now, he was furious, not so much because he opposed the theme park but because he had sold his land much too cheaply.

Except for their united support of stagnation, the opposition included a mix of otherwise rather strange bedfellows. The law-abiding sawmill owner Gus Gammon was shoulder to shoulder with the notorious poacher, Wilbur Findlay. The wizened pianist at Falling Waters Church, Thelma McCracken, was chumming it up with the tone-deaf Durwood Green, impresario of Karaoke Night at the Sunrise. Most astonishingly, there was orchard owner Caleb Barnes cozied up with cemetery sexton Digger Hanson. The two hadn't spoken for ten years, not since Digger buried Caleb's uncle in the wrong plot, but here they were, gleefully collaborating on creative insults to hurl across the bridge. Others on the team included an array of good old boys from the Sunrise, not noted for taking strong positions but reliably at the center of any local dispute.

As he surveyed the skirmish, Harry was unable to place Mal Grandbush in either camp, as the Belfry librarian was flitting from one end of the bridge to the other, snapping pictures with a tiny camera. Harry jabbed Nibber. "What on earth is she doing?" Just then, Mal backed up to the rail on the far side of the bridge and urged the combatants to look her way and wave.

"You don't know?" Nibber seemed surprised. "Last fall, without so much as a howdy-do, Mal up and appointed herself the official Belfry historian. If you'd been to the library lately, you'd know she has a bunch of scrapbooks all laid out on the reading tables. Pictures of 'most everything – Hurricane Clara, the Christmas Village Stroll, the burning of The Grand."

"Well, I'd say there's another entire album coming," Harry said as he caught sight of Henry McLaughlin, arms outstretched along the top of the rail, looking very much like a boxing referee. At first, Harry thought poor Henry might be trying to calm things down, but of course it was by then well into the afternoon, and the man was almost certainly well into his cups. There he stood, on wobbly legs, playing the role of an interpreter of sorts, magnifying and repeating insults from one group to the other, stirring the pot, causing even more trouble.

On the fringes of both wings were a number of non-combatants, clearly enjoying the battle, loudly cheering every point and counter point on both sides of the divide. The ruckus continued for several minutes until Jeff Molony suddenly went on an especially fierce screaming tirade, only inches from Horatio's whiskered face. The startled crowd fell silent.

"You're just like the rest of 'em." Molony wagged his finger under the old man's nose. "You do nothing but crab about the sad state of affairs around here, but when something comes down the road that might help us out, you fight it tooth and nail." He moved in even closer. "You're nothing but a gawd-damned hypocrite!" The "p" in "hypocrite" sent off a glistening spray of spit.

Despite Molony's proximity, it was apparent that Horatio hadn't heard the specifics, and his face took on a puzzled look. Poor Henry saw his chance and quickly sidled up to Horatio, cupped his hands, and yelled straight into his better ear. "He says you're nothin' but a gawd-damned Democrat."

Some in the crowd began to giggle, but Horatio instantly flew into a terrible rage. His cheeks took on an even deeper shade of red, and the blue veins on his temples jumped out like roads on a map. He lunged forward as fast as one could in hip boots, lifted the poke oar high over his shoulder, and took a mighty swing. The weapon cleared the shorter man's head by a foot or more, but the momentum sent Horatio careening onto the far side of the bridge where the oar cracked to an instant stop against the concrete rail. The shock sent Horatio sprawling onto the sidewalk, where he clutched his left shoulder and writhed in pain. "You no good son-of-a-bitch!" he screamed up at Molony. "I'll get you. You just wait!"

Molony doubled in laughter, and Harry half expected his arrogance would start an all-out battle of oars, fists and fish rods, when suddenly the entire mob grew silent at the startling, single whoop of a siren. Deputy Kelly Hallowell had arrived in her white sheriff's cruiser. She parked crossways in the road, light bar flashing, and members of both teams, some already in hasty retreat, made a necessarily wide berth as she waddled her way to the center of the bridge.

"Okay boys, there's enough!" She smacked her nightstick in her gloved hand and growled. "Party's over. Go on about your business, or you'll sure as hell wish you had." She pretended to reach for her holstered pepper spray, but the gesture wasn't needed. Half the crowd had already scattered up the road to Knight's or back to their boats. Others slipped out of sight the second she reached for the mace. Molony and Rafferty lingered just long enough to let the deputy know they weren't afraid of her, then walked back to Rafferty's black Hummer, parked above the dam. As the vehicle drove past, Nibber raised his hand in a friendly wave, but Rafferty ignored him and kept his eyes straight ahead.

"Stuck up snot," Nibber mumbled, at once reducing his wave to a single, large finger. "Someone ought to sugar up the gas in that Hummer hog of his."

Harry chuckled and looked back across the bridge. The only person left was poor Horatio, still flopping on the sidewalk, trying frantically to shed his rubber waders with one hand. Nibber walked over to offer him some help, but was greeted with a snarl, and he returned to the sheriff's car where Harry and Winston had gone to wait. "Geeze," Nibber said, eyes wide, "the guy's a little bit touchy. And, just because he thought someone called him a Democrat."

They watched as Horatio at last managed to get his waders hoisted over his good shoulder and begin to make his way down the bank where his aluminum boat was tied to a rock on the edge of Mosher Stream, above the dam. The cracked poke oar made a loud boom when he slammed it onto the bottom of the boat. The noise made Winston jump, and he cocked his head cautiously as Horatio clambered into the stern, started the old Johnson with one pull of the rope, and slowly motored up the stream toward home. Harry wasn't sure if the white mist hanging over the boat was caused by having too much oil in the gas or by the steam of Horatio's rage.

"Too bad," Harry said after the man disappeared around the first bend. "He's really a nice old guy, just got a bit het up by the tongue-lashing from Molony. He'll get over it, but he doesn't like that guy, and he truly hates the idea of Pond Park."

"I'm glad he doesn't have far to go," Nibber observed. "Lord knows where the poor soul will live when Grunwald sells his place and reclaims that cabin at the head of the stream. Horatio loves the place. Been renting it for years."

"It's not *if* Fritz sells it," Harry said. "It's *when* he sells it, and right there's another good reason why Horatio is so dead set against Pond Park."

Deputy Kelly waited for the entire crowd to evaporate, and then beckoned the waiting vehicles across the bridge. Winston ran to show her his approval, Harry and Nibber close behind. "Well done," Harry said, gripping her chubby hand. "You got here in the nick of time. The lid was about to come off."

Kelly shoved her nightstick into her belt. "John phoned me from the store," she explained. "Said a bunch of guys had been fishing and minding their own business when somebody called somebody else a name. After that, you know how it goes, one thing led to another." She hunched her shoulders and tugged at the bottom of her coat. "I should have arrested the whole lot of 'em."

"For disturbing the peace?" Nibber wanted to know.

"Nah," she said. "Ever since that sign went up, there's been no peace to disturb." She gestured up the road, toward the store. On the right was a large new wooden sign, white with red letters. In their haste to catch the battle on the bridge, Harry hadn't noticed.

COMING SOON
BELFRY LAKES PARK

Roller Coaster	Water Slide
Carousel	Miniature Golf
Dark Rides	Flying Elephants

"I don't get the flying elephants part," Nibber shrugged. "Or dark rides, for that matter."

"Me neither," Harry replied, "but I'm guessing dark rides are what we're in for."

3

Kegels

Harry sauntered through the door and had just plopped a bag of take-out on the kitchen table when he was startled by the sounds of heavy breathing at the other end of the big, open room. He turned to have a look, and his jaw dropped. Diane and Nibber were on their backs on the carpet, legs spread wide in front of the glass doors facing the lake, making strange grunts and gasping noises. Winston was beside them, on his back as well, his tongue lolling and all four legs churning the air.

"Would somebody please tell me what's going on here?" Harry asked, nervously. "I run out for a few minutes to get supper and come back to find my living room has turned into a gymnasium." He paused. "Or a brothel."

Nibber waited to catch his breath. "Kegels," he finally panted.

"Kegels?" Harry was mystified. "What's kegels?"

"It's an important exercise," Nibber explained. "For expecting mothers. Strengthens the pelvic floor."

"Good lord, so how come you're doing them?" Harry asked. "And Winston?"

"Oh, they're just coaching," Diane offered. "You know Nibber. He's quite read up on the business of having babies, and very attentive, as you've noticed." She reached to scratch Winston's belly. "Winston, too."

Harry wasn't about to follow up, but Nibber was. "I picked up a pamphlet on kegels at the hospital when I took Diane for her check-up last week," he said before shifting to detail. "She's almost two centimeters, you know. Won't be long." Harry groaned.

"He also picked up a traffic ticket," Diane giggled, nodding at Nibber. "Thought he'd turn the trip to Watford into a trial run, just in case the baby comes when he's on duty," she explained. "He was calculating the travel time, right down to the second, and we were nearly at the hospital when some guy in a big SUV cut us off on South Street. I don't know what got into him, but all of a sudden Nibber got it in his head that the baby really *was* coming. He laid on the horn and we took off like a Banshee." She giggled some more. "Boy, I'll tell you, that old Chevy of his can really *move*. When we got into the emergency room parking lot, there was a blue light behind us."

"Yeah," Nibber jumped in, "and for what it's worth, I thought the guy was quite rude. Just because the woman wasn't actually having her baby, he didn't have to be so snippy."

Harry pulled the Styrofoam containers out of the paper bag; two with generous portions of meatloaf and onion rings, one with meat scraps for Winston, and a green salad for Diane. At the bottom of the bag were napkins, plastic forks and a dozen or more packets of salt and catsup. "Debbie put this all up for us at the Sunrise," he said, proudly. "Else we'd never have gotten so much. She said to be sure to hold the Whoopee Pies until she got here after work." He shot a warning glance at Nibber.

Over supper, Harry asked Nibber a number of gynecological questions, and the three speculated over whether they might get their state trooper friend, Aidan Brown, to fix the speeding ticket. They were almost finished with the main course when Debbie be-bopped through the door, threw her coat over the empty kitchen chair, and tugged at her clingy sweater. "How's the mama and the papas?" she wanted to know.

Nibber and Winston scrambled to their feet to greet her, and Harry lunged for his water glass to keep it upright. "Mama and *papa* are quite fine, thank you," he said. "And, why wouldn't we be? We've got an unemployed obstetrician right here in residence, not to mention a Golden Retriever who thinks he's a midwife."

Nibber brushed at a blotch of catsup on the front of his Dam Committee tee shirt and gave Debbie a suffocating hug before latching onto her shoulders and holding her out at arms' length. "Nice tips." he said.

Harry wasn't at all sure it was a question. Diane knew it wasn't. "That'll be quite enough," she said, pointing Nibber to his seat.

Debbie's face reddened, and she wagged her head, making her long black ponytail flip from side to side. "The tips weren't bad for a Sunday night," she said. "Not as good as the summer people, but local folks do what they can. Wilbur Findlay doesn't tip me at all, but he sometimes brings deer meat. Makes me think, there's a package of frozen filets in the car."

Debbie settled into her chair, and Diane passed out the Whoopee Pies. "Turns out, it was a good thing there wasn't much of a crowd tonight," Debbie sighed. "Folks made me seat them in separate groups, with empty tables in between. People who favor Pond Park were mostly in the middle, under the wagon wheel chandelier. The rest took tables around the edges. Even the rowdies at the bar were split up, with an empty stool in the middle. I'm tellin' you, you could have cut the air with a knife. I don't know exactly what happened up by the dam yesterday, but it must have been some wild affair. Somebody needs to fill me in. When I got home late last night, Nibber wasn't interested in talking." She blushed again.

Harry was eager to oblige, and he raised one hand, palm out straight ahead to keep Nibber from butting in. He went over the full proceedings, from the moment he and Nibber and Winston got to the dam, to the grand finale when Deputy Kelly arrived to break things up. When he finished, he went on at some length about Horatio, "hopping in hip boots like Kermit the Frog," and told of the man's somewhat violent reaction to poor Henry's purposeful misinterpretation of Molony's name calling.

"Imagine," Nibber said, "all in a snit because he thinks someone called him a Democrat."

"Well," Harry explained, "people around here are funny about these kinds of things. Try telling Hummer at the post office that Rush Limbaugh is nothin' but a fat windbag, and then see what happens. He'll about crawl over the postage meter to grab your throat."

Diane had heard the complete episode before, but she followed along intently. "Goodness me," she said. "Horatio at the Bridge. Now, that's really cute."

Harry and Nibber swapped puzzled looks. "Greek to me," Harry shrugged.

Diane laughed out loud. "Not Greek," she corrected. "Roman."

Still swamped, Harry moved on. "All this commotion about Pond Park has turned the village upside down," he said, gravely. "I wish there was some way we could put the kibosh on the whole thing."

Diane nodded. "Maybe somebody could prove Rafferty torched The Grand," she said. "If that happened, the insurance company would come after their money in a flash, and then there's no way the developers could afford to build Pond Park."

Harry admitted it would be good for justice to be done, but he wasn't sure it would halt the project. "I'm guessing the real backer is the Black Wharf mob," he said. "Those guys have got tons of money."

"All of it dirty," Nibber jumped in, flicking a brown crumb of Whoopee Pie off his shirtfront. "We're barking up the wrong tree here, anyway," he said. "As far as proving arson is concerned, Deputy Kelly says the state people conducted a thorough fire investigation. Rafferty and Molony were both most definitely in Boston that night, and besides, there hasn't been a trace of evidence that the fire was deliberately started."

"What say we focus on trying to stop these outsiders from getting approval to build that awful park?" Diane asked as she jammed a pillow behind her back and shifted to get comfortable. "If anybody thinks the ever-lasting garage sales around here are terrible, imagine what it will be like having a permanent carnival, smack in the middle of town."

"So, let's sort out where things stand," Harry said as he began to rehearse what they already knew. In the first few years after the hotel was closed, the owners sold off a couple of parcels of land along the road to pay the taxes. The scheme didn't raise enough money, and they soon gave it up. Last fall, when Ned Rafferty and his backers bought the hotel to fix it up, the road properties weren't needed, but after the hotel burned and they came up with the plan to build Pond Park, the highway department insisted they acquire more land near the road for safe access and parking.

"That's why Jeff Molony conned Gabe Brumbley out of his place awhile back," Nibber jumped in, "and that accounts for the *"sale pending"* sign we saw on Fritz Grunwald's lawn yesterday. That lot slopes gently up to the site of the playground. Turns out to be the only place that works."

"So," Harry said, resuming his role as moderator, "we come to the special hearing next Tuesday night." He explained that the acquisition of the Grunwald property was the final step in the permitting process. "However," Harry said, "while the town expects the Department of Environmental Protection to sign off, it hasn't happened yet, and now the opponents of Pond Park have convinced the DEP to hold a special public hearing for the airing of more environmental concerns."

"What could they possibly find?" Nibber wanted to know. "Spotted owls?"

"Probably not," Harry said, "but there is a question about wetlands. The low end of Grunwald's property goes down to Finger Lake, but as the proponents point out, they don't need to use that part if all they want is a place to get in up above and park cars."

Harry summed up. "Here's the deal," he said. "The local scuttlebutt has it that Rafferty's sales agreement with Grunwald is based on having all of the necessary permits issued. There's no sense in them buying property if they can't use it. If the DEP finds a reason to deny permission, the Grunwald property doesn't sell and Pond Park is dead. It's a long shot, if you ask me, and there sure isn't much time."

Diane folded her hands across her swollen belly. "Do you think someone else could jump in and buy Grunwald's property to keep it away from the mob?"

Harry shook his head. "Probably too late for that," he said, "and even if it was possible to break the purchase agreement with Rafferty, who would buy it?"

"We could," Diane said calmly. "We still have money left from Doc O'Neil's suitcase." The room grew quiet. Standing over his water bowl, Winston stopped mid-slurp. Nibber put a finger in each ear. Harry looked around the table, scowling a warning. They were the only ones who knew the full story.

One night last spring, Harry and Nibber had stumbled onto Doc O'Neil's murder up on the ridge, beyond Nibber's cabin. On the way home through the snow, they discovered a suitcase, filled with money. Within days, the word was out that Doc had been the head of Boston's drug dealing Black Wharf Gang, and he'd made off with the profits. Before long, lots of people were out looking for the drug money, including gang members and the Feds, who claimed it was government property.

The four of them – Harry and Diane, Nibber and Debbie – faced a dilemma. If they kept it for themselves, they would surely get caught the minute they suddenly blossomed out with new and unaccustomed riches. If they turned it in, all the money would simply disappear and not do anybody, certainly nobody around Belfry, a lick of good. In the end, they agreed to keep it and put it to good local use. If, in the process, the money turned out to improve things a bit for themselves, so be it.

Now, half of the money was already gone, anonymously donated to all sorts of local projects. Early on, nobody was the wiser, but when Doc's murderer got caught the previous Labor Day, things changed. By then everybody was certain the money was somewhere around town, but nobody was sure who had it. The four decided to hunker down, and they hadn't spent a nickel of the tainted money all winter long.

Harry broke the silence, and turned to Nibber. "So, exactly how much money *is* left?"

"Gee, I donno," Nibber said. "Been meaning to count it, but haven't had time. Not to worry, there's plenty enough to do what we want. In the meantime, don't worry, it's all safe and sound." Harry looked at Diane, who was nodding in satisfaction. At first, they'd kept the suitcase overhead in the Crockett garage, and it made her nervous. Now, the suitcase was gone and the cash was in bags. Diane had convinced Harry to let Nibber take care of it. It was Harry's turn to be nervous.

The money was moved soon after Debbie moved into Nibber's cabin. In preparation for cohabitation, Nibber made a few renovations that included the discontinuation of the tiny half-bath off the kitchen. He'd shut off the toilet and put the money in several plastic bags in the drained tank. Harry thought it was a terrible hiding place, but didn't complain for fear it might end up back at the Crocketts'.

"Anyway," Harry said, getting back to the notion of them buying the property, "there are a couple of things wrong with that idea. First, how on earth could we keep the money secret if we suddenly came up with a bag of tens and twenties to buy the place?" He knew there was no answer for that, and moved on. "I'm pretty sure Fritz wouldn't sell it to us, anyway. He'd be afraid of ticking off Rafferty and Molony, not to mention the thugs behind this playground project. He's a very jittery and nervous man, as we all know."

Diane agreed. "Poor Fritzy is so nervous he makes *you* look like the Dalai Lama."

Harry shrugged. He didn't know the Dalai Lama. "Never mind," he said. "I know Fritz pretty well, and I'll make it a point to run into him and feel him out."

The discussion abruptly ended at the strains of *Bridge Over Troubled Water*, Harry's telephone ring selection. Nibber marched to the coffee table and picked up. "Crockett House," he said, "Mr. Nabroski speaking."

Nibber's playful grin evaporated at once. "What say?" He waited. "You sure?" Another pause. "OK, fine. Be right there."

Harry got to his feet, and peered into Nibber's face. "That was Deputy Kelly," Nibber explained. "There's a body of a man fetched up at the dam. They need us to go and narrow up the gate so's they can snag it out."

4

No Bolony

The day had been especially warm and with the cooling afternoon temperatures, a thick fog shrouded the village and made it hard to see. Nibber turned on his windshield wiper and the driver's side was clear in a single swipe. The blade in front of Harry merely hiccupped. "You really should get this damn thing fixed," Harry crabbed.

"Don't really need to," Nibber replied. "Never use it."

Harry harrumphed and cranked down the side window. Winston hastily crawled into his lap, and together they stuck their heads out into the damp air. Up ahead, blue lights cut through the mist and eerily reflected off the white buildings on Main Street. As they approached the bridge they could see the winking red taillights of the Belfry rescue truck, blocking the right lane, back doors swung wide open.

Nibber pulled left to sneak by, but Deputy Kelly was very nearly filling the entire open lane. He waited, and when she recognized the Chevy she moved aside to let them pass. At the other end of the bridge was Henry McLaughlin, doubtless pressed into service to help coordinate the alternating single line of traffic. Poor Henry seemed a bit confused, and he slowly twirled the STOP and SLOW pole sign in his hands, unsure of which side to display to the oncoming traffic. Nibber drew up close, and Harry spoke out the window to Henry. "Who is it?" he asked.

"Henry," Henry answered quickly. "Henry McLaughlin, at your service." He was wearing Kelly's Cebennek County Sherriff's Department baseball cap that he must have swiped from the cruiser. It hadn't been properly adjusted, and it covered nearly all of his forehead and both of his ears. Harry leaned out the window and thought he caught the fumes of recycling Jack Daniels. Winston did too, and he stretched even farther out the window to lap poor Henry's flavored face. Instinctively, Harry pulled his head back in. "I *know* perfectly well who you are," he barked impatiently. "What I meant was, who is it that's in the water."

"Oh, that." Henry looked even more confused. "I have no idea," he said, pausing a second before he pointed cheerfully to his pilfered cap. "And even if I did, I couldn't possibly tell you."

"God almighty," Harry mumbled, waving Nibber on, "Kelly gave him instructions on everything except how to direct traffic."

Nibber pulled into a small parking space on the far side of the bridge, near the hand-lettered, unauthorized sign that he'd put up himself: *For Dam Officials Only*. Harry left his window open and explained to Winston he'd have to stay in the truck.

Once back on the bridge, Harry looked off to the left, into the water where the outlet stream from Grand Pond broadened out to make a large pool that spread across the dam and its spillway. Although the surface seemed calm, beneath, the water was racing to the dam before it made a seven-foot plunge into Finger Lake.

On the left bank of the pool, the moving water had carved a small gravel cove where fishermen could launch small boats. A few had already been put out to their buoys, tethers stretched by the current, sterns stiffly facing the bridge. Harry could now see several men gathered up on the narrow beach. One of the men spotted them and scrambled up over the rocks and jogged over. Will Colchester, chief of the Belfry fire department and rescue squad, was grim-faced and all business. He nodded at Nibber. "You need to close the gate a bit," he said. "We'll have to quiet the water some so's we can float the body away from the dam." Nibber had left the Tainter gate wide open for a number of days, managing the spring run-off. The roar of the water was deafening.

"Whose body?" Harry fairly screamed.

"Donno." Colchester shrugged. "The man's upside down." He paused a second. "Anyway, I couldn't tell you if ...."

"I know, I know," Harry cut him off, "you couldn't tell me if you knew." No sense in pressing Will Colchester. He'd managed the scenes at most every chimney fire and fender bender in Belfry for the past twenty years. Even the cops obeyed when he gave an order.

Nibber reached into his pocket and fished out the garage door clicker he'd rigged up as a remote control for the dam, but Harry shook his head. "Oh, no," he said. "You know I don't trust that thing. Best you go down and run the gate properly, from the box." Nibber seemed tempted to push the button, anyway, but instead he turned and headed out along the slippery catwalk on the opposite side of the bridge.

Harry ventured toward the rail to peer underneath, but he wasn't ready to look, and he headed for Deputy Kelly, still at her station, directing traffic and shooing gawkers off the bridge. Kelly was the one who had started all of the "need to know" business in the first place, soon after she joined the Cebennek Sheriff's Department. But, since last fall when Harry gave her the clues and the credit for solving the murder of Doc O'Neil, the rotund officer had been somewhat more willing to share police secrets. "Who is it?" Harry asked innocently when he drew near.

"I honestly don't know," she replied, sounding as if she might be willing to tell him if she knew.

Harry went back to look along the launching spot and could now see that State trooper Aidan Brown was there, standing with several rescue workers, giving orders. A number of the volunteers were holding long poles fixed with grappling hooks. On the opposite bank and away from Kelly's guarded perimeter, a small group of spectators were huddled together, pointing toward the scene and shading their eyes as they peered into the floodlights. Suddenly, seemingly out of nowhere, Malvine Grandbush appeared on the rail, next to Harry.

Harry jumped. "Holy smoke, you scared me," he said. "How on earth did you get out here, anyway?"

"I told Deputy Kelly that I have press privileges," Malvine said, waggling her tiny camera. "History's being made of the dark side of Belfry, right here and right now."

She put her face square in front of Harry. "People have a right to know, you know."

"I do know," he said.

Eyes sparkling and cheeks flushed, she pointed under the bridge. "Who is it?" she asked wistfully, brushing at a damp grey curl that dangled from beneath her floppy hat.

"Don't know," Harry said with a wry grin, "and I couldn't tell you if I did."

Colchester broke up their conversation when he yelled across the dam to Nibber, whose head was lost in the control box. "There's a plenty," he hollered. "Hold it right there." The groaning of the Tainter gate suddenly stopped, and Harry went to the edge once more. The current had slowed a bit, and Harry watched as three men slowly waded into the stream and reached out with their poles. Two of them turned back when they had gone as far as they could. The third pressed on until the water sloshed over the top of his chest waders, causing him to panic as the sudden added weight made it impossible to move. The first two turned and held out their poles to haul him in. Colchester cursed them from the bank. "Get back here," he ordered. "We don't need to be pullin' out more than one body at a time."

The first two climbed out and flopped the third onto the banking, head down, toward the stream, and waited for the water to drain from his boots. Meanwhile, Colchester began fixing one of the iron hooks onto the end of a long rope. While they waited, Harry glanced at the floating body for the first time. It was a man, to be sure, short and stout, seeming to be curled up in a ball, legs drawn up and arms wrapped around his chest. He wore blue jeans and Bean boots, and a tattered and faded orange life jacket, its straps buckled, covered his red, plaid shirt. His bald head glistened in the floodlights.

At that moment, Nibber arrived from the other side, and they watched as Colchester swung the tethered grappling hook over his head several times before letting it fly. On the first toss, the iron claw landed with a thump atop the life jacket.

"Ouch," Nibber exclaimed. "That's gotta hurt." Harry turned to agree, but Nibber was already gone, scurrying over the rocks and down the banking. He reached the bottom just as they hauled the body onshore and flopped it over. Colchester bent down immediately and began administering CPR, but it was easy enough to tell it was a waste of time. Even from where he stood, Harry was sure the man was dead, and he was also quite certain he knew who it was. Within seconds, both of his thoughts were confirmed when Nibber looked up and caught Harry's eye.

"It's Bolony," he gasped, using his favorite nickname before regaining reverence. "It's Molony," he said properly. "Jeff Molony." He glanced down at the body quickly, then back up at Harry. "Deader 'n a hake."

*****

Harry's head swirled with speculation as he slowly walked back to the truck to retrieve Winston. *Jeff Molony! Dead? How?* The dog made a grand, wailing celebration of the reunion, and he followed Harry smartly at the heel as the two headed back over the bridge where Kelly was still standing, talking on her radio. She held up a hand to muffle Harry, who could hear the crackling voice of Aidan Brown on the other end. Kelly listened intently, interrupting only to say "10-4" a half-dozen times before she clicked off and put the radio back on her hip.

"That was Trooper Brown," she announced to Harry. "Gave me a 981 and a 10-55, and then said we might possibly have a 187." Harry frowned, and she translated. "The 981 says to resume normal traffic, which I'm doin' right now. A 10-55 is a case for the medical examiner. Brown will take care of that. As for the possible 187, I think you probably know that would be a suspicion of a homicide."

Harry didn't know. "You don't say?"

"I'm gonna have to wait for someone to come from the Attorney General's office," Kelly explained. "Maine doesn't trust local cops with suspicious deaths. It'll take a while for one of the hot-shots to get here from Augusta."

Harry took one last look under the bridge. The body was on a flat place along the bank, covered with a blue tarp. The rescue team had already packed their truck, and Will Colchester moved it up the road. Kelly beckoned poor Henry to surrender his traffic post, and then opened both lanes, shaking her nightstick at the occasional driver who slowed to gawk.

The day's warmth had brought on the first crop of spring peepers, and a chorus of the tiny frogs echoed in a single high-pitched scream out of the backwaters along the stream. Winston sat with his chin resting on the bridge rail and cocked his head this way and that, mystified by the constant chirping. Within seconds the howling sound of the water cascading over the dam returned. Nibber had re-opened the Tainter gate, and he and the nosy librarian soon joined Kelly, Harry and Winston by the rail.

"So," Harry ventured, looking at Kelly and then gazing up the stream toward Grand Pond. "What do you suppose?"

"It's one of three things," the deputy said with an air of certainty and obvious pleasure at being asked. "It's either an accident, a suicide, or a murder." They waited to hear her selection, but she disappointed. "As for which one it is, your guess is as good as mine."

"Well, I can tell you something right now," Nibber said. "It most certainly wasn't a suicide. That man thought far too much of himself to do that sort of thing."

"Besides," Harry shrugged, "a man bent on drowning himself doesn't put on a life jacket first."

"Anyway," Kelly said, "whatever happened, he didn't jump off the bridge. One of the Knight kids – I don't know which one – saw the body floating toward the dam about 6 o'clock. It was coming from somewhere up toward the head of the stream. The kid ran to the store, and John Knight called us."

Strangely, Malvine had yet to say a single word, and Harry began to wonder if the excitement had been too much for her. She finally broke her silence. "Most likely," she said rather sadly, "it was a plain, old-fashioned accident. As interesting as it might be to have this turn out to be a murder, I'd have to guess the foolish man went out in his kayak and fell overboard. It's that simple. He's been out most every afternoon for a couple of weeks, ever since the ice started breaking up. 'Course he lives on Finger Lake, but he keeps his kayak on the Grand Pond side, almost exactly where he's laid out at this very moment."

The conversation quickly turned to the question of how long a person might survive in cold water, and ended when Kelly firmly stated she knew from her training that in water below 40 degrees, a man could die in an hour, even without drowning.

Nibber shivered and crunched his hands deep in his pockets. Malvine picked up where she'd left off. "Come to think of it," she said, "Horatio Perkins was in his runabout at the end of the stream at about five o'clock, but I never saw Jeff Molony at all."

Kelly's ears perked up, and she rummaged in her puffy jacket for a notepad and pencil. "Did you say you saw Mr. Perkins in his boat?"

Malvine seemed pleased to be questioned by the law, and she chose her words carefully. "Well," she began, "of course you all know I generally mind my own business."

Nibber snickered. "'Generally' is a very vague term. Perhaps you should give one or two examples?"

Malvine paid him no attention. "Everybody knows Horatio rents from Fritz, next door to where I live on the stream. It's hard not to keep track of his comings and goings. Oh yes indeed, he was out there all right. These eyes don't lie. I know what I'm talking about."

Kelly said she was duty bound to report the sighting, and was almost certain Horatio would be questioned in connection with Molony's death. "No way around it," she said. "If this thing turns out to be a murder, we've not only got Mr. Perkins near the scene, but don't forget, we've also got about two dozen witnesses to his threatening of Molony during the battle on the bridge."

Harry turned to Kelly. "Horatio wouldn't hurt a flea," he said, "and besides, what makes you think it was a murder, anyway? Whatever made Trooper Brown think it was necessary to call in the AG, in the first place?"

"That's quite simple." Kelly answered quickly. "If it was an accident, and Molony fell out of his kayak, where's the kayak he fell out of?"

"Good point," Nibber agreed. "Those boats are near impossible to sink. You'd think it would have washed up with Molony."

Harry wasn't so sure. "Probably fetched up on a log," he said. "Besides, it's too dark to see anything up the stream. They'll find it in the morning, I'm pretty sure." His mind went back to Malvine's sighting of Horatio Perkins and the suspicion of foul play. He turned to Kelly. "Hard to imagine there's reason to suspect Horatio," he said. "The man just got himself cranked up a bit. After all, he really did believe Molony called him a Democrat. Who wouldn't get in a bit of a snit over that?"

5

Murder Capital

The medical examiner and the state's attorney had come and gone, and Harry, Nibber and Winston waited by the dam until the hearse was loaded before they headed up the road. It was well after nine o'clock, and Harry was surprised to see Knight's Store still open. Except in the short summer, the place usually closed promptly at seven, but tonight's discovery of a body at the dam had churned up a hungry and thirsty crowd. A few rescue workers were chatting under the gooseneck light at the gas pumps, and inside, they could see others milling around by the coffee urns and the beer cooler, everyone in animated conversation.

"We gotta stop and see what we can find out," Harry announced. Nibber agreed. Winston was anxious to get home, but his groan of protest was promptly overruled.

When they entered, Allie Knight was working the cash register, looking a bit bedraggled as she swiped a credit card for a single can of Bud. A few of her uncountable kids raced up and down behind the counter, squabbling over the remnants of a fast-cooling pepperoni pizza. Off to the side, Mal Grandbush stood on an empty milk crate, still snapping pictures. She jumped down the instant she spotted Nibber. "There you are, you poor dear," she gushed. "I really hate to bother, but when we were on the bridge just now, I forgot to ask you something very important." She fairly trembled with excitement. "You were so close to the body and all, and I need some detail if I'm expected to make a decent historical record. Could you tell me exactly how Molony looked when they finally fished him out?"

Nibber thought for a second. "Cold," he finally said. "Very cold. And kinda blue."

"You know that's not what I mean."

Nibber thought some more. "Well, I guess you can say he looked a lot like his old self."

"How so?"

"Well, for one thing, he was huggin' himself."

It wasn't the kind of description the historian was seeking, and she made a face of her own before moving off to get a picture of John Knight, standing in his apron in front of the ovens. John managed a half-hearted smile, then beckoned with his pizza peel to Harry, pleading for a rescue. Harry moved to wedge himself in front of

Malvine, and she scurried off toward the back of the store where some of Will Colchester's volunteers were earnestly re-enacting the toss of the grapple hook.

"Accident or murder?" Harry asked John. "What do you think?"

John scratched his chin. "Not sure," he said. "Probably an accident. I didn't care much for the son of a bitch, don't know anybody who did, but I certainly can't think of anybody who would actually want him dead. I'm sure I didn't. He spent a lot of money in here." John stopped to think some more. "Well, of course Horatio Perkins actually did threaten him. Lots of people heard it, but the Horatio I know could never murder anybody."

Harry agreed. "And besides, Horatio's not the only suspect." He winked at the storekeeper, and then pointed at Nibber who had just joined them. "As I recall the story, my friend here tried to kill Molony with a bottle of catsup one night not so long ago at the Sunrise."

"Oh, for God's sake, Harry," Nibber came back. "That was entirely justified. Bolony was threatening my livelihood as an electrician, making it out like I'd burned down the Belfry Grand."

John chuckled, and then pointed toward the fresh produce where Fritz Grunwald was standing by himself, back to and hunched over, fumbling with a cabbage. Harry and Nibber hadn't noticed before. "Ah, just the man I need to see," Harry declared.

"Bad timing," Nibber suggested.

"No time like the present," Harry shot over his shoulder as he made his way over to Grunwald, who was now absent-mindedly rolling the cabbage up and down the display bin. Harry tapped him on the shoulder, and the man jumped. "Jesus!" he yelled, turning around.

It was Harry's turn to jump. Grunwald was a total wreck. His face was an ashy gray, and his bulging eyes were rimmed in red. His mouth seemed locked on the edge of a scream. "Sorry to scare you," Harry said calmly, resting his hand on the man's shoulder. "I thought maybe we could have a word or two."

Grunwald wrung his hands and opened his stiff jaw, but all that came out was another Jesus.

Harry gently patted Grunwald's shaking arm and slowly made his way back to Nibber, who was having his second chocolate sugared. "Got one for Winston, too," Nibber explained. "Not chocolate, of course. Chocolate's not good for a dog. Got him a jelly-filled." He pointed to his coat pocket. "How'd ya make out with old Fritzy?"

"That man is some shook," Harry said. "All's he could say was 'Jesus.' Sounded a little like a tent revival meeting over there. I half expected him to break out into *Rollin' in the Deep* any second."

"He'll calm down," Nibber said. "You can catch him later. We gotta be getting home, anyway. It's not good to keep the girls waiting, especially with Diane in her current condition."

Nibber was fathering again. Harry cringed. "Look, I've gotta talk to that man. There are things we need to know about the sale of his property, and we're fast running out of time. Let's wait a few minutes; I'll try again."

The customers were thinning out, and Allie Knight stood twirling the ring of store keys at the cash. Harry walked over. "Seen Horatio Perkins?" he asked.

"He was in here about 3 o'clock," Allie said. "His shoulder was hurting him real bad, and I told him he should run in to the ER in Watford and have it checked."

"Anybody else in the store at the time?"

"Oh, the place was loaded. I remember because Jeff Molony cut the checkout line. Said he was in a hurry because he wanted to get out in his kayak. Needed a loaf of bread or something, and instead of lining up on the left like everybody knows they're supposed to do, he came barging in from the right." She shook her head. "People were some ticked off, I can tell you. Mal Grandbush had a hissy fit, and even Molony's good buddy Ned Rafferty told him he should be ashamed of himself. Hasn't been such a row since last summer when some guy from Boston took a swipe at some New Yorker who beat him to the last bottle of Tanqueray."

"Had Horatio left by that time?" Harry wanted to know.

"Nope. Course he wouldn't have been able to hear any of it, anyway."

Harry went on to tell Allie that Horatio could be questioned about Molony's death, and she seemed surprised. "So somebody actually does think this was a murder, huh?" She shook her head, and pointed a finger at Harry. "Do you realize that if this turns out to be a homicide, Belfry, Maine, will become the murder capital of New England?"

"Right up there with Cabot Cove," Harry admitted.

"Or El Salvador," Nibber added.

"El Salvador is not in New England," Allie said, "and as chair of the Belfry Business Group, I can assure you that this is not a funny matter at all. Murders are really bad for business." She turned around and began snapping off the lights. Harry asked her to wait. Grunwald hadn't strayed from the produce, and was now fidgeting with the oranges, all the while muttering quietly to himself. Harry and Nibber ventured over. This time, Nibber made the approach.

"Hey Fritzy," he said, trying not to startle him. "How's it goin'?"

Again, Grunwald turned and jumped with a loud "Jesus," but this time he looked as if he might have something more to say, and Harry took over.

"Gee, I can see you're all upset, and I'm really sorry. I know Jeff Molony was a friend of yours, and …

Grunwald cut him off, mid-sentence. "The lousy bastard was no gawd-damned friend of mine," he snapped. "If he was here right now, I'd wring his neck."

"I guess that would be what you might call over-kill," Nibber observed.

Harry was stunned by Grunwald's reaction, and he gave the man a quizzical look, urging him on. Grunwald looked cautiously around the store, and then, in a low whisper, began a long tale of woe. He explained that he hadn't been able to pay his taxes for two years and that the town was about to take over his property. He said he had planned to sell his place near Pond Park and move into his cabin on the stream that Horatio Perkins had been renting for years. "Six acres at my house," he explained, "including a crummy bit of shoreline on Finger Lake." He went on to say that when the final permit was issued on Pond Park, he was going to get one-hundred-and-fifty thousand dollars and out of debt. "Molony even promised to pay me in cash."

At the thought of cash, Grunwald forgot about whispering. He raised his fists, dropping an orange, and all but yelled. "And then what in hell d'ya think happened?" Neither Harry nor Nibber ventured a guess, and Grunwald roared his own answer. "The stupid asshole up and took his kayak into the cold water and drowned himself, that's what." His face was crimson. "Dumb, thoughtless bastard."

"Watch your mouth!" Nibber nodded his head toward Allie, standing by the front door, wide-eyed, still jangling her store keys.

"Don't suppose I could have a look at that agreement, do you?" Harry lowered his voice. He was on thin ice and he knew it, and he was surprised when Grunwald simply shrugged.

"Don't care one damn bit," the man said. "As a matter of fact, I got it right here." His hands shook as he pulled a folded and crinkled document out of his back pocket. One by one, Allie began turning off the store lights, and Harry suggested they move outside and let her lock up the place.

With Nibber two steps behind, Grunwald paced around the gas pumps while Harry stood under the light and glanced over the document. It didn't take very long, and he intercepted Grunwald on his third or fourth pass around the pumps. "This here agreement is pretty straight forward," he said. "As I read it, all it says is that when all the necessary state and local permits are issued, you will sell your property to Jeff Molony for the amount stated. It's a thirty-day agreement, signed by you and Molony on March 15. The only permit left is with the state environmental people. If they sign off before April 15, it's a done deal." He did some quick figuring. "That's still about two weeks away."

Grunwald gave Harry a wild look. "Yeah, but the son of a bitch is dead."

"Doesn't matter," Harry said. "Any lawyer will tell you, the agreement is probably binding on whoever's left. Maybe his wife, if they can find her."

"That could take forever. I don't have time."

"Well, I'm afraid you're stuck," Harry said, "unless, of course, things drag on and no permit is issued. Then the agreement expires, and you could sell the property to anybody you like." Harry edged closer. "Come to think of it," he said, "you wouldn't happen to be interested in selling the property to someone else, would you?"

The answer came quickly. "Oh, I couldn't possibly do that," Grunwald stated flatly. "Two reasons. First, there's nobody but the Pond Park crowd that wants the place, anyway. Second, I gotta tell you, I'd never even dare sell it to anyone else."

"Why not?" Nibber made his first worthy contribution.

"You guys don't know this Pond Park crowd," Grunwald replied. "They scare me half to death. That pug-nosed Rafferty is bad enough, but then there's some real bad boys back of him, running things in the name of Lake Land Creations, an outfit out of Massachusetts."

"Massachusetts? That figures." Nibber kept the stand. "And how do you happen to know all that?"

"Because," Grunwald explained, "last winter – the week before Christmas, as I recall – this guy I'd never seen before comes to the house and says he's friends of Molony and Rafferty. He was a real scary bastard, and a slick dresser. Didn't even take off his hat. Claimed to represent a Massachusetts corporation named Lake Land Creations and wanted to know if I was interested in selling the place.

I didn't tell him I was broke and that I had to sell; I just said I might. He said he was sure we could come to an agreeable arrangement, and that Molony and Rafferty were out of town at the moment but would come see me when they got back. I didn't agree to a damn thing, but he acted like it was a done deal. He grabbed my hand and shook it hard. If you could have seen his eyes! One real mean bastard."

"Have you seen that man since?" Harry inquired.

"Yup," Grunwald said. "A couple of days after I made the deal with Molony, he and Rafferty came to the house asking to see the agreement I just let you read." He pointed to Harry. "They passed it back and forth a couple of times, and then this other guy tells me that whether the agreement expires or not, I'm still going to sell the land to them, no matter what. If you could have seen the look on his face, you'd know he meant business. That's why I'm not about to deal with anybody else. No sense in me getting shot over the whole thing." The thought kicked off a new round of trembling and yet another "Jesus."

Harry probed deeper. "You don't happen to remember the name of this friend of Molony and Rafferty, do you?"

Grunwald thought for a long moment. "Corrado," he finally said. "Yeah, that's it. Corrado. Michael Corrado."

Nibber shot a glance at Harry. "Holy shit!" They both spoke at once. "The Nurse!"

"You know him?" Grunwald seemed surprised.

"Never met him," Harry said, truthfully. No sense in upsetting the man more than he was already, and there certainly was no profit in explaining that Michael "The Nurse" Corrado was the man who had taken over Boston's Black Wharf Gang when Doc O'Neil was murdered. Although nobody around the village could say they'd ever actually met the guy, everybody knew he'd been in town several times last fall, looking for Doc's suitcase filled with money.

6

The First Miracle

The air was warm and still all night long, and in the early morning the last thin carpets of ice shattered into millions of tiny pieces and whooshed to the bottom of the lake. Within hours, the game wardens were out in force, scouring the length of Mosher Stream and out into Grand Pond, looking for Jeff Molony's red kayak.

The day began with a startling page-one headline in the *Watford Journal:* **Dam Death Declared Suspicious**. The story said that, pending a full report from the state medical examiner's office later in the week, "officials are treating the discovery of the body of the well-known Belfry realtor as a suspicious death." It went on to say the authorities were asking the public for help in finding Molony's missing kayak and that meanwhile an autopsy was being conducted in Augusta.

The news was startling enough by itself, but after lunch, when word spread that the searchers had come up empty, the village became rife with speculation and rumors. Those who held to the notion that Molony had simply fallen overboard were unable to explain the missing kayak, leaving the door wide open for others who much preferred to believe the man was murdered. Among those who favored homicide, not surprisingly, was the librarian-historian Mal Grandbush, who now seemed convinced that Molony was wiped out by an out-of-town hit man, hired by one or two of the anti-Pond Park people. While not many subscribed to her wacky theory, the tie-in with the theme park controversy contributed to the general excitement and edginess, up and down the line.

At Gammon's Sawmill, the latest gossip brought Harry no end of frustration as distracted workers threw caution to the wind and callously waved and shouted over the howling saws. On Tuesday, with the special town meeting set for 7 o'clock, Harry's safety responsibilities got harder still. By then, the sawmen and stackers had nearly forgotten about Molony and were instead sorting themselves out by Pond Park position, shoving and growling, stirring trouble on every shift.

When the closing whistle blew, Harry was relieved to find a bit of peace, and he rushed home to find that Nibber had gotten there ahead of him. His friend claimed he'd come early to check on Diane, but Harry knew he'd come for supper. Debbie was working the evening shift at the Sunrise, and Nibber didn't like to eat alone.

They were barely settled at the table when Harry began to fret. "I hope you know we're licked on this Pond Park business before we even begin," he said gloomily. "We're much too late in the game. There's nothing that can be done."

Nibber, at that moment using a table knife to baste a chicken thigh with catsup, was distracted by Harry's doleful pronouncement, and he splattered a generous blotch on the front of his Dam Committee T-shirt. "How so?" he asked, spitting on his napkin and spreading the red.

"Think about it," Harry said. "The agreement Fritz has to sell his property expires April 14. That's only ten days from now. If the DEP people give a permit before then, we can be sure the property will end up in the hands of the Pond Park people, never mind that Molony's out of the picture. Tonight, even if they decide they need another inspection, the whole thing is likely to be settled before the 14th. The only way I see of getting beyond that date is for them to find something on the inspection that causes even further delay." He shook his head. "Most unlikely, it seems to me."

Nibber picked his teeth with a tiny bone. "Heck," he sputtered, "all's we need is a few miracles. I bet we could come up with one or two if we tried."

*****

Susan Hanson had been crabbing for days about having to conduct the DEP meeting. After all, it had been only a few weeks since she was made to manage the raucous annual Town Meeting, and the follow-up work would have her swamped for weeks to come. Now, adding insult, she was expected to arbitrate between two village factions at war over a playground. To make her life even more difficult, for the past couple of days Town Hall had been crawling with investigators, using the place as a command center as they worked to sort out the mystery of Jeff Molony's sudden demise.

Hanson's misery found easy company with Mal Grandbush, who wasn't at all shy about telling anybody and everybody that neither one of them was being paid near enough for the work they were expected to do. It was Grandbush who gave Hanson the courage to rent the Belfry Grange for the special meeting without asking the selectpersons' permission, and it was Grandbush who encouraged Hanson to take the extra, unauthorized step of hiring Kelly Hallowell as stand-by security in the very likely event things got out of hand.

In fact, Deputy Kelly was standing just inside the Grange door when Harry and Nibber arrived, five minutes early. "Overtime," she grinned, patting her hip pocket before gesturing, usher-like, toward seats on the left side of the long center aisle.

"Cripes," Nibber observed as they headed down the center aisle, "this place is set up just like a wedding."

"What would you know about weddings?" Harry grunted before noticing that the friends of Pond Park were all seated on the right, and the opponents were all on the left. The two sides were at the moment alternately glaring back and forth at each other while mumbling with their teammates, waiting for the proceedings to begin.

Harry spotted a number of open seats about midway down the left side, and pointed them out to Nibber before he spotted Gabe Brumbley, seated all by himself, mid-row, an oasis of empty chairs all around. Harry knew why. Last month Gabe had bravely come out of the closet, and now he was being shunned by practically everybody in town.

For a long time there had been wide suspicion of Gabe's proclivities, but in mid-March, soon after the

Yankees took two straight from the Red Sox in spring training, all doubt evaporated when Gabe marched proudly down his driveway and slapped a Yankee sticker on his mailbox. His outing of himself caused a great uproar. It was one thing for the flatlanders to parade Yankee paraphernalia during the summer – they could simply be ignored – but it was quite another thing to have a Yankee booster in their midst the whole year round. So far as anybody could tell, Gabe was the only Yankee fan in town.

Local kids promptly dispatched the mailbox with a well-placed cherry bomb, but Gabe was determined. He replaced both the box and the sticker and, for good measure, sent away for an official Yankee cap that he was wearing at this very moment.

Although Harry considered himself broad-minded, there were limits to his tolerance, and he waved Nibber two rows farther down, to a couple of empty places on the aisle.

They had no more than settled in when manager Hanson rapped a gavel on a wobbly banquet table set up in the middle of the small stage. It was precisely 7 o'clock. Hoping to break the chill in the air, she began with an attempt at levity. "Did you know," she said, forcing a smile, "that this is National Tell a Lie Day?"

Nobody laughed. Nobody even said a word until Mal Grandbush jumped up on the left. "And you should all know that this is also National Librarian Day," she announced, proudly.

The sound of a scraping chair on the right announced road commissioner Bo Chilton, who got to his feet and pointed his finger accusingly across the aisle. "Yeah, and you people are no doubt about to observe the first one tonight. Meanwhile, we'll take care of honoring our fine librarian on this side."

Hanson's attempt at warming hearts obviously hadn't worked, and she at once banged the gavel to get down to business. "We are here because the Department of Environmental Protection has agreed to have a second public hearing on the matter of issuing the last state permit for the Pond Park proposal," she announced before explaining that the only real issue at hand was whether or not there were any overlooked environmental concerns about the Grunwald property that would prevent its use for an access road and parking for the park project. She made it clear that the hearing would last one hour, not one minute more, and then introduced the stranger at her side.

Clarence Wyman, she said after detailing his lengthy credentials, was the DEP hearing officer who would conduct the meeting.

Wyman rose confidently from his seat, his hand smoothing the only necktie in the room. His gray ponytail bobbed as he nodded politely up and down both sides of the Grange and thanked Hanson for her fine hospitality.

He then introduced his colleague. "Dr. Phoebe Highman is an experienced biologist in our department," he said, "and she will be the one to follow up in the event there is need for further investigation." Harry thought he sounded a bit doubtful.

Highman sat pertly erect, pencil poised over a notebook on the table in front of her. The thick lenses of her horn-rimmed glasses reflected the light and made it hard to see her eyes, but her cheeks were clearly flushed with excitement, and Harry sensed she was thoroughly enjoying her assignment.

Wyman tried to set the tone from the get-go. "Understand please," he said calmly, "that we must handle this meeting in an orderly fashion. Please wait to be recognized and, for the record, please give your name before you speak. Perhaps it goes without saying that we also must confine our discussion to those things over which our department has control under the laws of the State of Maine." He asked for questions. There weren't any.

He had no more than opened the discussion, when all of his rules were broken at once. Kerri Woods, owner of Belfry Lodge, began speaking before she was recognized, neglected to give her name, and wasn't about to limit her discussion. The plainspoken innkeeper glared directly at Wyman. "You people are paid to protect the environment, is that right?" Wyman nodded. "The environment in the village of Belfry is quiet and peaceful, is that not right?" Wyman nodded somewhat less vigorously. "So, tell me why you don't just do your job, deny the permit, and spare us all this foolish rigmarole." At that, she sat back down and looked around the hall in a most satisfied way.

It was easy to tell that Wyman had been in situations like these before. "That is a very fair question," he said with a straight face before he passed it off to Susan Hanson, who got wearily to her feet.

"Yes," the beleaguered town manager said, "but it is a question for the town to address, not the state." She then gave Woods's question another deflection by nodding toward Zac Dutton, chairman of the Belfry Planning Committee, seated with the opponents, in the middle, on the left side. For ten years or more, Dutton had spent endless hours crafting one set of town zoning ordinances after another, only to have them routinely and roundly rejected at each succeeding Town Meeting. The most recent version, greatly watered down, had been roundly defeated only two weeks before.

Dutton took his time getting to his feet. "As *you people* very well know," he began, pointing an accusatory finger around the entire hall, "the Planning Committee has been saying for years that we need a sound framework for future village development. Oh, but no," he said, disgustedly, "there isn't hardly anybody around here can even bear the thought that somebody might tell them what they can or cannot do with their own property." He paused to let the statement sink in. "Well, now it's far too late to stop Pond Park, and it's all your fault. You just wait and see, if we don't do something about zoning laws pretty soon, Belfry's gonna be faced with things a whole lot worse than Pond Park."

Henry McLaughlin was standing in the back with Deputy Kelly. "Like maybe pole dancing, or casinos," poor Henry tossed in helpfully. Both sides roared, and Hanson banged the table yet again. It was only 7:15, and the people running things up front were already looking edgy.

Next up was Mal Grandbush, and the general groaning from both sides was audible as she ponderously lugged a pile of photo albums up onto the stage and plunked them down on the table. "Right here," she said, pointing to the stack, "you might very well find evidence of endangered species. I'm not sure exactly which ones as I'm not an expert on these things, but since this whole fuss began I've made it my business to take a lot of photographs on the Grunwald property. If you people in Augusta examine them carefully, you might find something very interesting indeed."

Wyman was tongue-tied, kept his hands at his sides, but his sidekick Highman smiled sweetly and tentatively reached out to pat the pile of albums in a non-committal sort of way. She didn't say a word, but her gesture was good enough to send Malvine happily back to her seat.

The meeting wore on, carried forward more by the weight of opinion than fact. Time and again, Wyman found the need to re-state his rules. A few Pond Park opponents were quite sure the DEP had overlooked the fact that the Grunwald property included wetlands, and that they would most certainly require protection. Again,

Highman was eager to reply. She proceeded to give a longish technical description of wetlands, at the end of which she declared with absolute certainty that the property had none. "Pools of water after a rain," she sniffed, "don't make a wetland." She flatly stated they would just have to give up on that notion, and they did.

Harry was beginning to think the hearing was all for naught. It was already nearly 8 o'clock, and so far, they hadn't heard anything that would warrant another inspection. He turned to say as much to Nibber, when Wilbur Findlay suddenly jumped to his feet, identified himself, and asked to be recognized.

"We have overlooked a very important issue," the notorious poacher declared as he moved to the front, brandishing a fistful of papers. "This Grunwald property has a winter deer yard," he pronounced, "and deer yards are protected by Maine law." He waved a copy of a map that he marched directly onto the stage and proudly presented it to Wyman. "Right there, in the section I have circled," he pointed with his finger. "I've seen lots of deer there every winter, as many as twenty or thirty at a time. They're in a cover of about a quarter acre," he declared. "Can't see 'em from the road."

Findlay went on to explain that the Pond Park plan called for the clearing of trees in the area to make way for a parking lot. "It just can't be done," he said flatly. It appeared that he had wound up his presentation, but as he made his way back to his seat, he seemed startled to find himself staring into a sea of doubting faces.

"Look here," he said, this time making his case to his fellow Pond Park opponents, "I was down there just last week. The deer have started to move, but there are still a few hanging around. If you want another witness, you could ask Jeff Molony." He paused a moment to consider the unlikelihood. "Of course, I know you can't ask him, since the son-of-a-bitch is dead," he conceded, "but Molony was there all right, probably checking on the property. He saw them deer, too, but he probably would never admit it, seein' as how he wants to buy the place and all."

Having gotten tangled up in his tenses, Findlay decided to sum up quickly. "Anyway, I know the law on these things, and you can't mess with a winter deer yard. It's just not allowed."

In an attempt to recover credibility for Findlay, Gus Gammon rose from his seat and looked directly at

Highman. "Just so you'll know, ma'am, this man really does know the Maine fish and game laws."

Swift agreement came from the other side of the hall. "He ought to," Bo Chilton piped up. "At one time or another he's had most all of them read to him by Miss Dimble, here." The road commissioner pointed to the warden, seated in the back, who joined in the laughter.

Wyman and Highman took the moment to confer briefly behind the table. All the while, Hanson impatiently scrutinized her wristwatch. Wisps of damp hair seemed glued to her forehead, and she was raising her gavel to rap the session to a close when Wyman held up his hand.

"We were beginning to think we were going to hear no new evidence suggesting the need for further inspection of the property," he said solemnly, "until this last testimony from Mr. Findlay." He nodded appreciatively at Wilbur. "Dr. Highman and I agree that it would do no harm at all to delay our decision until we can investigate the suggestion that the property may indeed include winter habitat for white-tailed deer." Wild cheers from the opponents nearly drowned him out as he went on to explain that, in addition to further department research, there would be an on-site inspection of the Grunwald property the following Saturday at 10 a.m.

"The public is invited," he said, "as long as everyone behaves and stays out of the way."

The opposing sides headed for the exit, sticking close to their respective doorframes as they filed out of the hall.

7

Upsetting News

It was nearly suppertime, and Harry was washing up at the sink. Winston sat patiently, leaning on Harry's legs, eyes on the sideboard, expecting an appetizer. "Where's Nibber?" Harry wanted to know.

Diane replied from the big chair across the room. "Stopped by after lunch to make sure I was doing my kegels." She turned to catch Harry's face and giggled. "Says the baby will be here in ten days, for sure."

"God almighty, the man is obsessed with having *our* baby." Harry couldn't stand it. "At first, we worried he'd feel left out when the baby came. Now, we have to worry the poor tyke will grow up wondering about his parentage. "

"Actually, the real reason he came was to borrow your boat," Diane laughed. "I told him he could have it if he'd put the dock in first. He didn't seem to care; said he had no jobs today, anyway."

"So far as I can tell, he doesn't have jobs any of these days," Harry said as he looked out the kitchen window and made a face. "He didn't put the dock in straight. That would make three years in a row."

"He was in a bit of a hurry, but he'll be here any minute, and you can tell him. Told me he'd be back in time for supper."

"I'm sure he did," Harry muttered over his shoulder as he and Winston went out the lakeside door. "We'll wait for him by the water."

Winston raced on ahead, down the slope and out onto the wobbly wooden dock, his tail wagging, eyes begging for a stick. Harry found one and hurled it as far as he could. The dog launched himself a full six feet off the end, churned his way to the stick and paddled back through the cold water with a wide "welcome spring" grin on his face.

Harry was set to wind up for a second toss when he heard the unmistakable whine of his Mercury outboard engine, and he turned to watch as the boat rounded the tip of Herman Point, bearing down at full throttle. Nibber hadn't bothered to adjust the trim, and the empty bow of the small Whaler porpoised, slapping hard on every wave. As the boat drew up to the dock, Nibber turned it smartly and sidled in sideways. Harry reached to grab the line, and Nibber cut the engine before he plunked a chewed-up plastic bucket and a long-handled fish net on the dock.

"I found it!" Nibber exclaimed triumphantly.

"Found what?" Harry eyed the bucket, covered with a grimy towel that seemed to bounce up and down of its own accord.

"Not that," Nibber shook his head. "I'm tellin' you I found Molony's kayak."

Harry did a double take. "Where?"

"North Bay." Nibber vaulted onto the dock, gave Winston a hug.

"I certainly hope you didn't touch it."

"'Course not." Nibber looked up, disgusted. "I'm calling Deputy Kelly to have her come real quick. There's still time to go get it before dark."

All three ran to the house, where Nibber caught Kelly on the first ring. "Wants us to get some rope," he said when he hung up. "She's bringing Warden Dimble. Said to meet them on the dock. Can't take Winston, she says. It's a crime scene, and he's likely to mess things up." Winston gave Nibber a dirty look before he flopped down disgustedly in front of Diane's chair.

"Hold supper," Harry said, taking a coil of heavy rope off its peg by the door. "Hard to know just how long this might take."

Nibber removed the bucket and net from the dock and set them in the shallow water near the shore, then turned the boat around, bow out. Harry slid behind the wheel just as Hannah Dimble came down the bank, Deputy Kelly huffing and puffing a few steps behind. They were on the water in seconds, headed up the lake.

The afternoon sun made a show of red and gold in the streaky western sky, and all around the shore the hardwoods displayed the new green of spring. Harry hadn't been on the pond since last fall, and taking in the sights and gulping the fresh air made him momentarily forget their mission. His reverie came to an abrupt end as they neared the south end of Loit's Island and Nibber jabbed him in the ribs, pointing to the narrow gap leading into the big part of the lake.

Harry slowed the engine to maneuver the marker buoys, and Kelly took the quieter moment to ask Nibber what on earth he was doing up in North Bay in the first place. "The water flows the other way," she said. "Seems an odd place to go searching for the kayak, if you ask me."

"I wasn't really lookin' for the kayak," Nibber admitted. "I was out searching for frogs."

Harry turned, made a face. "Frogs?" Nibber liked frog legs, said they tasted like chicken, but it was pretty early in the season to be chasing frogs.

Nibber leaned into Harry's ear, clearly not wanting the others to hear. "I'll explain it to you later," he said. "Maybe."

"That's a definite maybe," Harry shot back before dropping the subject.

It took a full ten minutes to cross the choppy open water, and when they reached the narrow shortcut into North Bay, Harry traded places to let Nibber drive. Here, near the inlet stream coming from the chain of lakes above, the pond was shallow, and the spring freshet was making visible swirls of current as the water sped out of the marsh.

When they reached the far shore, Nibber raised the engine to avoid the weeds, and the propeller sputtered as they skirted along the edges toward the half-hidden passage that led into the stream. Careful to stay in the clear, fast water, Nibber followed the twisting route for several turns until they came to a wide pool, carved by the current. Nosing the boat to the near side, he cut the engine, raised it out of the water, and snatched a paddle out of the thwart.

"We'll poke in from here," he said. "It's not far." He shoved the paddle deep into the mucky bottom, holding the boat steady for a long minute as he stared into the forest of dried brown cattails. "Right there," he said finally, pointing to a place no more than a couple of feet wide, where the tails had been flattened and oddly bent inward. He pulled the paddle out of the mud and let the boat drift in that direction.

"Stop!" Kelly demanded as they neared the opening. "I need pictures." Nibber pinned the boat again, and Kelly began to click. When she was finished, Harry took the second paddle and helped Nibber shove the boat into the tiny slot. The hull caught up on the stubborn, bending weeds, and with the stern sticking out into the moving stream, it was hard to keep the boat straight. They had moved in barely the length of the Whaler when Harry caught the first glimpse of red.

Kelly made them stop again, and while she took more pictures, Hannah struggled into her chest waders. "This thing didn't end up here by accident," Harry said as they stared at the now quite visible half-submerged kayak. "Somebody went to a lot of trouble to hide it."

"And it might have panned out for them if I hadn't found it," Nibber said with a tinge of pride. "Another few weeks and the new shoots would have hidden it for good, even from the air."

Hannah grabbed one end of the coiled rope and eased herself off the bow, settling another six inches after her feet hit the loose bottom. The silt grabbed her feet on every step, and it took a while to slosh her way to the kayak and fasten the rope onto its rear toggle. Once back at the boat, she tied the other end to the bow cleat before she climbed in and ordered Nibber to back the boat into the stream.

The kayak made a sucking sound when it gave way from its resting place, and they waited until they had hauled it out into the clear water to have a closer look. Nibber took up the slack in the towrope, and they were able to see plainly that the kayak had been struck on the right side, near the cockpit, in front of the seat. The blow had shattered the fiberglass, almost to the middle of the craft, now kept afloat only by its air pockets, fore and aft. Harry tugged the rope to bring the kayak even closer. Tiny flecks of pale green paint were evident along the full line of the fracture, where the glass had been scraped down to the cloth.

"Hit by a light green boat," Kelly announced. "Aluminum, I'd say."

"Crestliner, if you ask me." Nibber knew his boats.

Harry knew instantly what the others were thinking: Horatio Perkins owned an old Crestliner, a fifteen-footer, pale green.

It didn't take long for Kelly to let on that she was on the same track. Taking her radio from its belt clip, she signaled the Augusta barracks and asked the dispatcher to put her through to Trooper Aidan Brown. "Meet you at the Perkins' boathouse at the head of Mosher Stream in a half-hour," she said when he answered. "Better bring that AG investigator woman with you." She went on to give him the details of their discovery, peppering her conversation with police codes. "We've got ourselves a 187," she said, "and soon we may have a 10-15 as well." She clicked off and then translated. "A murder," she said, "and soon maybe a suspect in custody, as well."

****

The sodden kayak wallowed behind the boat, lurching from side to side as they hauled it back across the lake. Harry shortened the towrope, but it didn't help. It was nearly dark when they entered the marked channel at the end of Loit's Island, and Nibber took care to keep the red buoys close on the right as he headed toward the shore, where he slowed to a crawl as they made their way to Mosher Stream.

The long trip had given Harry time to work up a considerable fret, and he turned in his seat to ask Kelly how she could be so sure that poor old Horatio was a murderer. "Plain as day," she said. "Horatio threatened Molony. You heard it. Right there's the motive. And you know damned well we're gonna match Perkins' boat to the damage on the kayak." She pointed out the back. "So, right there's the weapon."

"That's not nearly enough, all by itself," Harry said flatly.

"Maybe not," Kelly came back. "But, don't forget Malvine Grandbush can place Perkins at the head of the stream at about 5 o'clock."

"So what?"

"What you don't know is that the medical examiner's report came out this afternoon." Kelly seemed pleased to be an insider. "He puts the time of death near 5 o'clock. Better than that, he says in his report that the death probably occurred at the head of the stream."

"How on earth would he ever know a thing like that?"

"Because," Kelly said, "he determined Molony had been dead about an hour before he showed up at the dam. On a calm day, even in the fast water, it would take about that much time for a body to float down from the head of the stream, that's why."

"Pretty clever," Harry admitted. "But, I still have a hard time making out Horatio as a murderer. Don't care what anybody says."

Kelly ignored the thought. "And by the way," she continued, "for what it's worth, Molony froze to death. Hypothermia. Didn't drown. No water in his lungs."

"I guess that doesn't really matter very much," Harry observed.

"Certainly not to Molony," Nibber chipped in as he began a wide turn into the stream, the kayak sloshing back and forth, behind.

It was only the first quarter of the new moon, but in the dim light Harry could make out Trooper Brown, standing at the corner of Horatio's boathouse next to the state's attorney they'd seen the night Molony's body was recovered. The woman moved quickly down to the water to catch the bow of the Whaler. She was tall and trim, and her dark hair was pulled back in a knot. She gave a stern look as she motioned everyone out of the boat. "Name's Jackie Johnson," she said abruptly. "I'll take over from here." She was all business.

Harry looked around. The entire area had been cordoned off with a yellow CRIME SCENE plastic ribbon. Standing in the shelter of her own front porch, in the next house up the stream, was Mal Grandbush. Even in the moonlight, Harry could tell she was fuming.

Trooper Brown helped Johnson pull the kayak out of the water and they turned it upside down on a patch of gravel. Johnson took a quick look at the damaged craft, and then motioned Brown to the open door at the back of the boathouse. Kelly went in with them, but when Harry and Nibber tried to follow, Johnson turned and shook her finger. "Stand back!" she ordered. "Police business."

The three officers went inside with their flashlights. Nibber waited to hear their footsteps on the narrow catwalk that spanned the width of the boathouse, then beckoned Harry to join him in the shadows by the door. Brown was holding a light while Johnson knelt at the bow of Horatio's pale green boat. Nibber nudged Harry and pointed. Sure enough, the keel showed streaks of red running from the front of the bow to the waterline. Kelly took pictures from every angle and then, wearing gloves,

Johnson removed a blade from a bulging black canvas attaché case and began to scrape, first on the green, then on the red, separately putting the particles in plastic bags that she promptly sealed and handed up to Kelly. The work was done in a minute, and Harry and Nibber were made to scramble back where they belonged.

The three uniforms next headed for the kayak, now high and dry, where Harry knew Johnson would continue her scraping. "Now's a good time for us to have a good look at that boat ourselves," Harry whispered. Nibber produced a penlight from the array of tools he kept in the deep pockets of his pants and, with an eye on the now otherwise-occupied investigators, quietly crept into the boathouse.

The stern was facing out the big open door at the water, and there was enough light to see that Horatio's Johnson was tipped up onto its mounting bracket and flopped to the side. The tiller was folded, and a tattered seat cushion, its ties still twisted in the form of the knots that once held it, had been removed and left in a puddle of water under the right seat.

"You're looking at the wrong end of the boat," Nibber whispered. "All the interesting stuff's up here." He was bent over the bow, examining the damage with his penlight.

"Let's go," Harry said, all of a sudden. "We've seen enough, and I want a word with Mal Grandbush before we leave."

Kelly was just coming from the shore, and Harry waved her over. "Where's poor Horatio?" he asked.

"He signed the consent form for a search and simply shrugged." Kelly chuckled at the thought. "Told 'em to have themselves a good time and then he headed off to the meeting of the Pond Park opponents that's being held up at Falling Waters Church. I 'most forgot about the meeting, but I suppose it was all pretty calm if none of the proponents showed up."

Kelly excused herself, explaining she needed to arrange to have Horatio's boat picked up and impounded, and Harry and Nibber walked the fifty feet to the Grandbush house, next door.

Mal was still standing on her porch, only inches from the yellow ribbon. Close up, Harry could see that, sure enough, she was steaming. "Hey, Mal," Harry said, trying to be nice. "Where's the camera?"

Her face turned red, even in the moonlight, and she was trembling with rage. "That hussy witch took it away from me," she hissed, pointing at Johnson's backside, just then disappearing into Brown's cruiser. "You'd think, for gawd sake, that this was North Korea or somethin'."

Harry thought it best to change the subject. "Would you mind telling me again about seeing Horatio in his boat last Sunday night?"

Mal seemed pleased to be needed once again. "Well," she said, pointing over her shoulder to her kitchen window, "I was at the sink, making supper, and happened to see him leave the boathouse. Not that I'm a snoop or anything like that," she explained, "but you always have to be looking. Can't trust your own ears, and sometimes I can't hear his engine unless the wind is blowing just right."

Harry nodded vigorously to get her back on track. "It was late afternoon," she said. "Horatio's been going out about that time for several days, since even before the ice went out of the big lake, fishing for humpback perch near the head of the stream. Brought me a mess last week. Fried 'em in salt pork, with corn meal. Absolutely delicious."

Harry peered in close, his eyes begging her to skip the recipe. "Well," she said, picking up the thread again, "he made a couple of slow trips across the inlet and then, on the last trip, he was heading straight at me when he suddenly picked up speed and turned sharply inward, toward the stream, and reversed direction. I watched him real close on that last turn because it made the boat list heavy to starboard. For a second or two there, I thought for sure he was going to take on water, but he didn't. He righted himself with no problem."

"I'd say he wasn't trolling for perch at that point," Harry observed. "What else?"

"Well, you see I had a cake in the oven," Malvine explained. "I went to take it out and when I got back to the window, he was gone."

She was played out. No more to tell. Harry patted her arm, and he and Nibber headed back to the Whaler.

"I'd have to say, old Horatio Perkins is in a pickle," Nibber offered when they were out of earshot. "When the state lab report comes back on the paint samples, they'll have him in cuffs before you know it."

"Maybe so," Harry admitted, "but when the cops come to the door with a warrant, a guilty man usually doesn't greet them with a shrug and merrily head off to a protest meeting." Nibber nodded mild agreement, and neither spoke until they reached the water. "In any case," Harry said as they began shoving the boat away from the shore, "guilty or innocent, that man is going to need a good lawyer."

"How about Tony Pasquale?" Nibber suggested. "We thought he did a fine job defending Salome O'Neil at the murder trial last fall. He's retired now, but he still works some. Lives by himself on Loit's Island. I see him once in a while at Knight's, getting supplies. There's phone service out there. I'll call him and see if we can set up a meeting. We could pay him from the toilet."

Harry couldn't think of any reason to argue. "You do that," he said.

8

Flush with Cash

Harry paced nervously around the mill machinery all afternoon, struggling to keep his focus on OSHA regulations while at the same time pondering over the upcoming meeting with Tony Pasquale. If he and Nibber were not able to convince the wily attorney to defend Horatio Perkins, the poor guy was very likely to go to jail. He might go down, just the same.

Harry learned of the meeting shortly after lunch when Constance Paine, office manager at the Gammon Sawmill, suddenly appeared at the top of the stairs above the debarker, flashed the overhead signal light, then stuck her fingers back in her ears. Harry spotted her from his station and waited for the last few logs in the batch to rumble out of the feeder before he called a temporary halt. It was rare for Miss Paine to make an appearance on the operations side of things. She didn't much care for the saws, and she positively hated the growling debarker. Harry was afraid something was terribly wrong, or maybe the baby was on the way. "Is it Diane?" he asked the moment he reached the top of the stairs.

"Oh, no," the woman answered primly, "It's Nibber."

"Nibber?"

"He called just now and insisted I give you a message. Highly unusual, I must say. Interruptions cost money, as you know." She pointed to the silent debarker. "He wants you to meet him at his cabin after work," she said, leaning into Harry's face as if to inspect his teeth. "He also said he'd have the *mouthpiece* with him, whatever on earth that means."

Harry relaxed. Somehow, Nibber had convinced Tony Pasquale to have a meeting. "Thanks," Harry said. "And by the way, would you mind calling Diane and tell her I'll be late?"

"She already knows," Miss Paine sniffed. "Nibber said he'd stopped by at your house after lunch. Something about needing to do exercises. I have no idea what that means, either."

*****

Harry punched out promptly at 5 o'clock and headed off to Nibber's cabin. The string of warm days had thawed the ground, and road crews had already removed the FROST HEAVE signs from along the highway. He made good time until he turned off Shore Road and began to climb Nibber's long, gravel driveway where, half way up, he confronted a raft of wild turkeys, nonchalantly crossing the road, single file. He waited, and then impatiently blasted his horn at the last bird, a tom, which made a great ruckus in his startled flight to the nearest tree.

As he crested the ridge, Harry was greeted by yet another surprise, the latest in a long stream of upgrades at the cabin that began last fall when Debbie first moved in with Nibber. The skeleton Chevy pick-up and several discarded snowmobiles were sold for junk early on, and then the porch floor was cleared of trash and painted. In the late fall, a plant box was installed under the kitchen window and filled with green boughs and winterberry. Now, Harry was looking at yet another startling change. A forlorn pair of wooden lawn chairs, long hidden behind the cabin, had been moved out onto a tiny patch of pine needles that Nibber called his lawn. They had been repaired and sprayed a very shocking canary yellow. And, that wasn't the end of it. When Harry got out of his truck, he saw that the window box also screamed the same color.

So too, the front door, which seemed to be a bit tacky when he knocked.

"Hey," Harry said when Nibber came to the door. "You could have used some masking tape." He pointed to the splattered door jam. "And, where'd you get that wild yellow color of paint?"

"Masking tape doesn't allow you to blend the colors," Nibber replied. "And that yellow was left over from another project."

"What other project?"

Nibber wasn't at all interested in paint. "Come in," he said, "and meet Tony Pasquale."

The large man was seated at the kitchen table in front of the window. He was decked out for fishing: unlaced wading boots, zip-leg pants, and a tan chamois shirt under a vest neatly adorned with a colorful array of tied flies. A mosquito net was rolled onto the brim of his outback hat, its strings doubling as a harness for magnifying glasses that were perched on his broad belly.

Pasquale's knees cracked as he got out of his chair and reached to shake Harry's hand. "How do?" he said.

"We met once before," Harry said. "At the trial of Salome O'Neil."

"Oh, yes," Pasquale replied, although Harry could tell he didn't remember.

Harry turned to Nibber. "So, have you had a chance to explain to Mr. Pasquale the reason for this meeting?"

"Nope. I waited for you. We've been talking about the Pond Park disaster. Tony here really hates the idea." Nibber was already on a first name basis.

"Well, that's good," Harry said without further exploration. Instead, he turned to Pasquale and got down to business. "We think Horatio Perkins is about to be charged with the murder of Jeff Molony, and we'd like it if you'd agree to defend him."

Pasquale chuckled, shook his head. "Oh my," he said, "I'm sorry, but I'm all done with handling that kind of high-profile case. Takes way too much time. I'm retired, or at least working at it. I've moved out to Loit's Island. Doing a lot of fishing. I practice just enough law to get by. Wills, contracts, divorces. Stuff like that."

Harry pressed on. "Trouble is, we truly believe poor Horatio is innocent, although the cops think for sure they've got the goods on him. He won't stand a chance without a smart lawyer. You wouldn't want to see an innocent man go to jail, now would you?"

"Well, no," Pasquale admitted, "but you don't understand how complicated these things can get. It takes time and lots of money – and I'm pretty sure Mr. Perkins doesn't have much money."

"How much would it cost?" Nibber jumped in.

Pasquale seemed to be leaving the door open. "Five grand. And that would be just a down payment."

Nibber never flinched. "Do you take cash?"

Pasquale broke into a broad grin. "I do take cash," he said. "In the past, lots of my clients, especially the drug dealers, used to love to pay me in cash."

Instinctively, Harry cringed. There was never any doubt but that Doc O'Neil's lost money came from the sale of drugs. He glanced over Pasquale's shoulder at the door leading to the tiny discontinued half-bath off the kitchen where lots of that drug cash was hidden in the now disabled toilet.

"Can we stop right here, just for a minute?" Harry silenced Nibber with a glance, then turned back to Pasquale. "Let's just make believe that you agreed to defend Perkins and we gave you five grand in cash. Would you in any way be obliged to tell anybody where that money came from?"

Pasquale didn't hesitate. "Not unless you guys were somehow paying for a crime," he said. "Otherwise, I never ask any of my clients where the money comes from, and I don't tell anybody if I know."

"You wouldn't even tell Horatio Perkins?"

"Not even Perkins. I'd let him think I was doing it out of the goodness of my heart." He laid a hand across his broad chest.

Harry probed some more. "So, Nibber and I would definitely be protected in an attorney-client sort of way."

Pasquale cocked his head. "Well, now that you put it that way, not exactly. In this make-believe case, Mr. Perkins would be my client, not you. But even so, I'm telling you the money part would be safe with me."

"I take it you might be thinking about accepting the job?" Harry was hopeful.

Pasquale thought some more, and then nodded. "I'll defend the man for a five grand cash retainer and the promise of more if I need it. No contract. A handshake. No further talk of the money."

Nibber had been listening carefully, and he jumped in to clarify. "Of course, for the moment at least, this is all hypodermically speaking."

Nibber was clearly hung up on drug lingo. Diane, the Grammar Queen, wasn't around. Harry stood in. "That would be *hypothetically* speaking," he said, nodding at Nibber. "Why don't you and I step outside and see if we can make it real?" He got up and headed for the door. "Mr. Pasquale, you make yourself at home."

"There's really nothing to talk about," Harry said when they got outdoors, testing the paint on one of the lawn chairs before deciding to stay on his feet. As long as they could be sure the money secret was safe, all four of them had agreed to pay for Horatio's defense out of the toilet. "Still," Harry said, "it can't hurt to give the man some time to think."

"Pretty sharp guy, isn't he?" Nibber said to pass the time.

Harry agreed. "Add some hair, shave off about twenty years and forty pounds and the guy could be a model for the LL Bean catalog."

"No, no," Nibber said." I mean he's some sharp lawyer."

"Maybe he is, and maybe he isn't," Harry said. "In any case, I trust him to keep his mouth shut about the money. Let's give it to him and get on with it."

They stood quietly for a minute or two more, watching as the slowly setting sun turned the sky a shimmering red, then headed back into the house. Pasquale was just settling back into the kitchen chair. "Hope you don't mind," he said, "but I had to use the bathroom." Harry's eyes popped, and he sucked in his breath. "Gosh," the lawyer went on, "there's a lot of clutter in there. The place looks like a pantry. Had to move a pile of cans to get at the toilet and then, for some reason, the damned thing didn't work. Somebody turned the water off. I had to turn it on again before it would flush."

Harry cocked an ear. He could hear the toilet, still running. Nibber bolted for the old bathroom door. "Gotta go," he said over his shoulder. "Real bad."

Harry raised his voice to cover the squealing sound of the water shut-off. "We've decided to go ahead with the deal," he said to Pasquale. "Once my friend gets out of the bathroom, we'll give you the money."

Nibber was gone for a very long time, and Harry turned the conversation to Pond Park, allowing as how he was delighted that Pasquale was against the idea. The lawyer was apologetic about not making a public stand. "I've got village clients on both sides of this affair," he said, "and there's little enough business around here without me ticking anybody off."

Finally, Nibber emerged from the converted bathroom, looking sheepish and shuffling along like a two-year-old with a load in his pants. Harry caught on quickly. The money was stuffed in his trousers. He was willing to have Pasquale know they had some cash, but he wasn't about to let on where it was hidden. "Back in a second," Nibber said as he sashayed by the table. "Gotta run out to my truck."

There was another long pause before Nibber returned carrying two slightly damp plastic bags. "It's all here," he said, handing them to Pasquale. "Five grand, in tens and twenties. Count it if you want."

The lawyer took a red bandana out of one of the half-dozen pockets in his cargo pants and wiped the bags. "No need," he said. "I trust you, and I'll get right on the case. I guess I'll talk to the AG's office tomorrow and see what's cooking. If they plan to arrest Mr. Perkins, I'll try to have a chat with him first."

"Tony and I have been talking about Pond Park," Harry said, a little surprised by his own use of the first name. "I've been telling him how we've been trying to figure out a way to buy the Grunwald property out from under the Boston mob." Pasquale folded his hands over his chest and listened intently as Harry recited the facts.

"Molony's agreement to buy the land hinges on getting final approval from the environmental people," Harry explained. "The agreement expires on April 14, just over one week from today. If the permit is issued before then, the jig is up. Pond Park will be a go. There'll be nothin' to stop it."

He paused to let his point sink in. "I presume the fact that Molony's dead has little to do with it. One way or another, the Grunwald piece is gonna end up with Lake Land Creations, anyway?"

It was a question for the lawyer, and Pasquale nodded. "I presume you're right. And, you have to believe that after things get sorted out, Molony's heirs will be in cahoots with that bunch."

"Okay," Harry went on, "so right now the permitting is hung up waiting for a final DEP inspection, two days from now, on Saturday. Unless they find some reason for further delay, the permit is likely to be granted within the time limit of the agreement." Pasquale nodded again.

"Stay with me," Harry went on. "This thing gets more complicated. First, Fritz is absolutely terrorized by the Pond Park people and probably won't dare to sell to anybody but them, in any case. He's convinced Pond Park is controlled by a Boston mob, the Black Wharf gang, and we have our own reasons to believe he's right." Harry decided not to explain that Grunwald had told them of a visit from a thug that he and Nibber knew as the Nurse.

Harry let out a sigh. "And finally," he said, "there is the question of how we'd go about acquiring the property in any case, seein' as how we'd rather not be identified as having that kind of money."

Pasquale looked down and fiddled with the dry flies on his vest as he thought for a long minute. "What you boys need to do," he said finally, "is to fight fire with fire."

"How's that, Tony?" Nibber was interested.

"Make your own corporation." Pasquale smiled. "They're hiding behind one; you get one for yourselves. That way, you'll be ready to move if everything else falls into place, which," he added, "seems to me to be a rather unlikely possibility."

"I don't suppose you could make one of them LSD things for us?" Nibber was still talking drugs.

"Well, I suppose I could. It's not a whole lot of work. Just takes a visit to the Secretary of State's office and filling out a few papers."

"Let's do it." Nibber smacked a fist into a palm. "And, maybe you could make it a twofer."

"Twofer what?"

"Twofer the five grand I just gave you," Nibber grinned, hopefully.

Pasquale laughed. "Why not? I hate the playground idea as much as you do. We'll call it pro bono work. I can get credit with the bar association for that."

Harry was eager to seal the deal. "And, what should we name it? They've got that crazy LLC, LLC. We ought to try to be at least as clever as they are."

"Why don't you just leave all of that to me," Pasquale said, his eyes twinkling. "I've got an idea."

The three shook hands, and Pasquale creaked to his feet, ready to leave.

"One more thing," Nibber put up a hand. "Maybe you'd be willing to help out with one more little thing." He fished in his jacket pocket. "I got this speeding ticket last week in Watford. It's ridiculous. I was just trying to get a pregnant woman to the hospital. Do you think you could fix it?"

Harry rolled his eyes, but Pasquale laughed out loud and held out his hand. "Why not?" he said. "Gimme."

"Great," Nibber said. "Just wrap the cost into the five grand and that'll make me an official client of yours, with all the rights and privileges of confidentiality."

9

The Widget Box

It was just after five when Harry got out of bed. Winston, who'd been sleeping on the carpet on Harry's side, jumped quickly into the warm place next to Diane. Harry tiptoed downstairs, then shuffled down . the driveway in his slippers to fetch the newspaper. It was spread out on the table when Diane, bleary-eyed, appeared in the kitchen a few minutes later.

"Long night," she said. "Couldn't get comfortable."

Harry patted her belly and pointed to the headline on the front page of Friday's *Watford Journal*. "This won't make you any more comfortable," he apologized.

DAM DEATH RULED MURDER
Belfry Man Held as Suspect

Diane seemed a bit startled, but the news was no surprise at all to Harry. Nibber had called just before midnight to say he'd heard from Pasquale, who told him the state lab had tied the paint on Horatio Perkins's aluminum boat to the wrecked kayak and that a warrant had been issued for Horatio's arrest. Harry was relieved to hear that the lawyer had been able to get to Perkins's place before the cops arrived and told the man to keep his mouth shut. Pasquale reported that Horatio seemed quite pleased to have the guidance and never once questioned the lawyer's offer of free services.

Diane leaned in as close as her stomach would allow and read over Harry's shoulder. The State Medical Examiner determined Molony died of "hypothermia due to extreme temperature," and the police investigation had turned up evidence of foul play in the manner of his death. The story explained "a Belfry handyman, Nikolai Nabroski, discovered Molony's missing red kayak Wednesday afternoon while hunting for frogs in the north bay of Grand Pond." It went on to say that evidence taken from the damaged craft led to a boat owned by Horatio Perkins, a Belfry resident living on Mosher Stream not far from where the body was discovered. Perkins had been arrested overnight, the report said, and, following an immediate arraignment, the case could be sent to the grand jury within days. Meanwhile, Perkins was being held in the Cebennek County Jail in Watford.

"Oh, dear me," Diane sighed. "Don't you think maybe we should pay the poor man's bail with money from the toilet?"

Harry said no. "We can't hide behind Pasquale on that one," he explained. Everybody knows Horatio doesn't have a plugged nickel and doesn't own any property, either. If someone suddenly came up with the bail money, the secret of our hidden pot of gold would be blown out of the water, so to speak."

Diane was still feeling sorry, and Harry went on. "If we're feeling bad, just think of old Fritzy. He's probably wringing his hands this very moment, calling out Jesus over his likely loss of Horatio's rent."

"Well," Diane said, brightening a bit, "I suppose it's only a couple of days before Horatio will either be free or held without any bail, in any case."

Harry agreed. "In the meantime, at least we can say all of this has made Nibber quite famous. Clip that article and put it on the refrigerator. The Frog Man and Debbie are coming tonight for supper."

They both turned back to the newspaper, and Harry pointed to the last paragraph of the story, where the Medical Examiner was quoted as saying it was impossible to determine the exact time of Molony's death because the

CPR given by the rescue workers had "interfered with the normal process of rigor mortis."

Harry looked up at Diane. "*Very* interesting," he said. "You can bet Pasquale will somehow be all over that interesting tidbit in a flash."

The article offered no other new information. It made no mention of the altercation at the bridge, nor did it say that Malvine Grandbush had reported seeing Perkins in his boat that same afternoon, near where Molony was presumed to have gone out of his kayak.

Harry folded the newspaper and gave it to Diane. "I'm gonna stop by at Knight's for coffee and a chocolate sugared before I go to work," he said. "Call Constance Paine at the mill if you need me. And, whatever you do, don't let Nibber call her. She hates going into the mill in the first place, and Nibber's messages seem to confuse her."

*****

Knight's was bulging with customers, and nobody appeared to be in any rush to leave. The lingering crowd didn't surprise Harry, but he was taken aback when he realized that everybody was acting real friendly and mixing together. Apparently, all it had taken was a murder to melt the sharp division of Pond Park positions. For a time at least, the locals seemed to be unified.

Outside, John Knight was bent over the innards of his pumps, fiddling with the price regulator and surrounded by a small army of kibitzers, including the Rev. Eugene Peppard of Falling Waters Church. Harry stood on the edge of the ring, listening as Peppard did his best to explain the need to hold a funeral for Jeff Molony. "He was a deacon of the church, after all," Peppard explained, "and whether anybody liked him or not has got nothing to do with it. The man at least deserves a decent burial."

His case wasn't selling well, and someone suggested Molony's former wife should be taking care of such details. Peppard wagged his head sadly. "She doesn't give a rip," he said. "Deputy Kelly got her phone number from the investigators, and I called her. She already knew her ex was ex. She told me to go ahead and hold a service if we wanted to, but she and the kids definitely wouldn't be coming."

No one seemed to be very surprised, and Peppard continued with his report. "She asked me if I would arrange to have him cremated – twice, if possible, she said

– and then send her his ashes, cheapest rate. She claims she has a special place she wants to put him."

"No doubt about that," someone allowed, "but there won't be enough ashes to be able to spread over all of the property he stole."

John closed the panel on the pumps, and Harry noted the price had shot up a nickel.

"OPEC," John sputtered.

"Bless you," the reverend replied.

Hummer Humbolt had left the post office unattended and was standing with Harry in the outer ring. "Okay, suppose we did have a funeral," he said to Peppard, "who would go?"

It was a reasonable question, and the pastor had a ready answer. "That's all taken care of," he explained. "I've run into this sort of thing before. Lorry Devine has friends who enjoy going to church for any kind of thing." Lorry, a golf widow, was well known in the village for her acts of kindness. In moments of trouble, she was first on the scene with chicken soup, and she served on almost every volunteer board, from the library to the cemetery. "When I get in a spot, I give Lorry's ladies a few bucks and they serve as official mourners," Peppard explained. "Some are really very good at it, tears and all." He took the moment to ask John Knight if he was willing to put a coffee can in the store to raise the necessary funds.

With the matter of a funeral settled, Peppard's acolytes dispersed, and Harry moved inside where customers were happily smiling and exchanging pleasantries. Allie Knight was at the cash register, chatting cheerfully with customers who seemed to be thrilled by the distraction of Belfry's second homicide within a year. There was talk of little else – not Pond Park, not even the weather. Only Gabe Brumbley seemed out of place, standing by himself in the corner by the ice cube bags, his Yankee cap on backwards.

Henry McLaughlin was remarkably clear-eyed as he paced in the liquor section, located near the register, where Allie could keep a close eye. Poor Henry was at that moment contemplating the day's selection while having a lively conversation with Malvine Grandbush.

For five days, since the Battle of the Bridge, Mal had been in a full manic phase, and it wasn't hard to hear her elevated voice throughout the store. For once, she seemed to be in line with the general consensus. Horatio Perkins was the murderer, no doubt about that, but Mal had added a personal twist.

"He was paid to do it," she explained to the group she had corralled by the coffee urns. "The man needed money, and there were plenty of people around willing to contribute in order to get Molony out of the way. They no doubt thought that with Molony out of the way, the Pond Park scheme would die with him. Whether that's true or not, poor Horatio was a hired killer, plain as day."

"How so?" Poor Henry had left the liquor and was standing nearby.

"Oh, well," Mal said, tickled to be in the spotlight. "If you bothered to look around, you could find the evidence right here in the store." She pointed to a coffee can on the counter near the cash register with a grease pencil label that said: ERADICATION FUND. "I've seen plenty of folks chucking money in there for days," she said, all puffed up.

Allie Knight had been listening quietly, but when Mal presented her final evidence, the shopkeeper lost her patience. "Good God almighty, Mal," she shrieked, "the Eradication Fund is for lake milfoil, not Molony."

*****

Nibber and Debbie were already on the porch with Diane and Winston when Harry arrived home after work. Diane was stretched out awkwardly on the chaise longue, and it occurred to Harry she would certainly need a hand when the time came to stand up. She and Debbie were having iced tea. Nibber was in a nearby rocker, sipping a longneck Bud and grinning from ear to ear, leaking droplets down his shirt. Winston was on his back, churning his legs in his own version of kegels, but he quickly bounced to his feet when Harry came through the screen door. Harry dropped to his knees to get his face washed before supper.

"Thank God it's Friday," Harry carefully held onto his brimming martini glass and gently moved Diane's legs to make a place at the foot of the chaise. "It's been a long week."

"I'll say," Debbie agreed. "Three double-shifts at the Sunrise, and another one tomorrow. I've got to cover for the boss, who wants to go to the DEP inspection at Fritzy's place. Emily Boulette is a big Pond Park proponent, you know, eager for a flood of new Sunrise customers."

"Been a busy week for me, too," Nibber chimed in.

"So far as I can tell," Harry responded, "the only thing you've done was go frog hunting and turn up evidence against the man we're trying our best to set free."

"Speaking of all that," Diane said, "I've got a question for the two of you." She looked at Harry, then Nibber. "Since you both don't seem to think Horatio Perkins murdered Jeff Molony, have you given any thought to exactly who you think might have killed him?"

Harry was set to answer, but Nibber jumped in. "Well, of course," he said. "There's plenty of suspects. Start with half the village that doesn't want Pond Park, and then add most of the rest who never liked Bolony in the first place. Right there's a ton of possibilities."

"I don't suppose you've considered narrowing the list a bit?" Diane asked.

"Wilbur Findlay is one," Nibber suggested. "Think about it. When Wilbur talked about being at the winter deeryard he claims is on the Grunwald property, he said he met Bolony down there early this spring. What was Wilbur doing there, anyway?" He didn't wait for an answer. "Poaching, you can bet." Everybody nodded, and Nibber went on. "And how come Bolony was there at the same time? It's not too far fetched to think he was spying on Wilbur to get the goods on him. What if Bolony threatened to turn him in unless the poacher gave up his fight against Pond Park? Now, there's a pretty darn good motive, right there."

Nibber wound up his theory with a self-satisfied smile, and Harry jumped in. "Possibly," he said, "but not likely. What about the Nurse?"

"The Nurse?" Nibber seemed confused. "How so?"

"To be sure, we've never met the guy, but we know from Fritz that he's been around. More to the point, we know the Nurse is ruthless as hell, a mob killer from all accounts. For him, rubbing out Molony would be like a walk in the park."

Diane shook her head. "But, the Nurse and Molony were in cahoots, both of them leaders in the Pond Park deal. Good friends, I'm sure."

Nibber had warmed to the idea. "Doesn't matter," he said. "Mob guys bump each other off all the time. Remember the Corleones in *The Godfather*," he said. "They offed their brothers and cousins just as if they were perfect strangers."

"Good point," Harry said, winking at Diane. "And, by the way, we've completely overlooked one of the best suspects of all."

"Who's that?"

"Our famous friend here, The Frog Man, Nikolai Nabroski." Harry chuckled at his own line.

Nibber looked hurt. "Gee, Harry, why do you keep bringing that old story we don't want to hear about up for?"

The Grammar Queen held onto her belly and laughed out loud. "Now Nibber," she said, pointing her finger, "you know you should avoid using prepositions at the end of a sentence. You've just managed to use three!"

Nibber shrugged. "Sometimes, you just have to," he said, instantly cutting his losses by two-thirds.

Harry held up both hands to stop the giggling. "Time to go inside," he said. "Sun's going down. Getting cold." He and Nibber hoisted Diane out of the chaise and they filed through the screen door into the kitchen. Harry flipped the switch for the light over the table, and it sputtered two or three times before it went out altogether.

"I think you've got a short there," Nibber said. "I can fix it." He ran out to the truck and was back in a flash, carrying his toolbox and a small carton of parts. Harry suggested turning off the power, but Nibber shrugged him off and climbed onto a kitchen chair. Diane waddled as quickly as she could to place newspapers under his feet before he stepped onto the table.

They all watched as Nibber disconnected the light and opened the junction box. "Don't you need a license to do that sort of work?" Diane inquired.

"Obviously not," Nibber said, looking down. He grinned to underscore his confidence and at that moment, his screwdriver hit a live wire, sending a shower of sparks down over the table. The house went completely dark.

"So, now we know the breaker works," Nibber said, still full of himself as he climbed off the table and felt his way downstairs to the circuit box. The lights came back on in a few seconds and Nibber returned to his post. When the job was done, the light over the table shone steady and bright, and the handyman stood on the table for a long minute, admiring his work.

"Well done, Nibber," Harry said. "Now tell me, where'd you get this box?" He pointed to the small, corrugated cardboard carton, filled with wire nuts and assorted electrical gadgets.

"Found it in the trash at The Grand the last day I worked there before the place burned down," he said. "I've kept it all this time. Just the right size for what I need."

There was a mailing label on the box, and Harry held it under the light to read. "Says here it was sent to post office box 681, here in Belfry," Harry said. "No name. Who's that, you suppose?"

"Well, if you think it's that snot Ned Rafferty, you're wrong," Nibber said. "He got number 268 when he took over the Belfry Grand, and, so far as I know, he's never changed it." He thought for a second or two. "I thought I knew 'em all, but I haven't a clue about 681. Hummer will tell us."

"Hummer won't tell you a thing," Diane said. "There's sure to be some postal regulation that forbids it."

Harry kept reading. "It's from the Acme Mining Company in Clinton, somewhere. The rest of the address has been torn off."

"Probably not Maine," Diane said. "No mining in Clinton, Maine. Not much manufacturing, either."

"Ohio, maybe?" Debbie suggested.

"Could be Arkansas, or New York, even New Jersey." Diane was full of them.

Harry had been deep in thought. He turned to Nibber. "I'd like to borrow the box for a bit, if you don't mind."

"What'll I use for my stuff?"

"I'll find you something even better," Harry said.

10

Clemmys Guttata

Nibber parked on the side of the road, and Harry peered intently across the way at a dozen or so locals gathered at the foot of Fritz Grunwald's driveway, prepared to join the final inspection that would determine the outcome of Pond Park. The warm and friendly feelings brought on by the murder of Jeff Molony had apparently chilled overnight, as many of the same people were once again divided into two separate clumps. Neither group was talking to the other, and neither one was very large.

"The nay-sayers have tossed in the towel," Harry muttered. "Our cause is dead in the water."

"Like Molony," Nibber quipped.

"Speaking of Molony," Harry said, "at least the pro-park people have somebody to replace him." He nodded toward the tall figure of Ned Rafferty, standing smugly at the front, arms folded over his chest like a drill sergeant. "With Horatio in jail, our side doesn't have a single soul to take over."

"Except for Mal Grandbush," Nibber chuckled, nodding in the direction of the librarian-historian, who was at the moment bouncing in and out of the two groups, taking pictures, gesturing madly, and talking a blue streak.

"Of course, neither numbers nor leaders make much of a difference, anyway," Harry rambled on. "They won't find a single reason to deny the permit, much less anything to cause a delay long enough to get us beyond the deadline on the sales agreement. We're sunk. Never mind Molony's gone to his maker, the gangsters will eventually end up with the last piece of the puzzle, no matter what." He heaved a long sigh. "They'll be laying the concrete for water slides and roller coasters before you even know it."

Nibber paid no attention to his ranting. "It ain't over until that thin lady sings," he said with an impish grin, pointing at the DEP biologist, Phoebe Highman, standing between the groups, clipboard in hand, a plastic smile pasted firmly on her pinched face.

Winston had grown tired of waiting and was clouding the window with his panting. Harry opened the door to let him out, and the dog led the way across the road to where Highman was beginning to spell out the ground rules. "You are all most welcome to be here," she said, turning her head from one side to the other, "but this is very serious business, and you must be sure to stay at least twenty feet behind me so as not to disturb anything we might find." She stopped to make an exception for Warden Hannah Dimble, and then went on to admit she was "extremely doubtful" they would find anything to keep the DEP from issuing the permit, in any case. The scattered applause among the pro-parkers was quickly stifled by a stern look of disapproval that did not change when she noticed Winston.

"I *suppose* it's okay to bring *that dog*," she said, scowling at Harry, "but you're going to have to make sure he behaves himself."

Winston scowled back. He was clearly hurt, and Nibber jumped to his defense. "He's not *that dog*; his name is Winston," he said as he surveyed both groups, "and you'll soon find he's much better behaved than 'most everybody else here."

"Well, fine," Highman sniffed, reaching across her flat chest to separate her camera from her binoculars before she slung a backpack filled with tools of the trade over her bony shoulders. "Now," she announced, "let's go look for that winter deer yard Mr. Findlay claims is down here somewhere." She beckoned Wilbur to move up front, and, like a kindergarten class on a field trip, the entourage slowly trudged into the woods.

They had gone barely fifty yards when Malvine Grandbush violated the no-man's land perimeter and crept up to within a few feet of the leaders. Face flushed with excitement, she waggled her camera this way and that, into the trees. "Look there," she said suddenly, pointing to a tiny bird that clung to a tall tuft of grass in an open patch up ahead. "Sedge Wren," she exclaimed. "Endangered species. Obviously has to be protected."

Highman turned and looked only for a second. "House Wren," she clipped. "*Troglodytes adeon.*"

Nibber muttered to Harry. "Troglodytes? She talkin' about us?"

"Woman knows her birds," Harry replied.

Findlay led the way another hundred yards toward the lake and into a large clearing surrounded by a grove of fir and cedar. "Right here," he said. "Most certainly a winter yard for deer."

Highman, Dimble and Findlay walked slowly into the opening while the others fanned out along the cover of trees and waited. Harry leaned up against an old pine and was scuffling his feet when his eye caught something shiny in the duff. He reached down to pick it up. "Cartridge," he whispered, showing it to Nibber.

"Yup, from a .243 Winchester, I'd say." Nibber didn't know birds, but he knew guns. "I just found a couple of those shells myself."

"Keep 'em in your pocket," Harry said, "or Warden Dimble will end up taking Wilbur away from here in cuffs."

The group waited for the trio of experts to skirt the entire opening. When they returned, Highman began to report her findings just as Malvine yelped once more. "Right there," she said, aiming her finger high into a dead pine across the way. "Now, there's a Bald Eagle's nest, if I ever saw one. Absolutely, positively cannot be disturbed in any way."

Highman didn't even look up; she'd seen it. "Squirrel's nest," she barked dismissively before continuing with her assessment. "I have to say, this is most definitely *not* a winter deer yard," she said, leaving no room for debate. "Have a look at the bottoms of the conifers. There's been very little browsing. There were deer here, all right; there's scat around, but they didn't stay very long, and it's pretty obvious they didn't spend the winter."

"Most likely they wintered over in Findlay's freezer," Nibber muttered to Harry, whose heart sunk at hearing Highman's conclusion. The last hope of saving Belfry from the playground madness was gone in an instant.

The divided group was set to leave when Highman suddenly announced that inasmuch as they were already near Finger Lake, they might as well confirm one more time that there were no concerns about disturbing any wetlands. Harry knew this wasn't going to work, either. Although Nibber had opened the dam well before the end of the spring runoff in the hope of creating a semblance of a wetland, the water level of Finger Lake did not go up enough to matter. The dam keepers at the other end of the lake had seen to that.

Nibber looked at Harry, knew what he was thinking. "Couldn't raise it very far," he said apologetically. "But still, you gotta laugh to think how we kept things flooded at the spillway, near Bolony's place. If that man was alive today, it would surely kill him."

Harry pondered the impossibility of what Nibber had just said as they followed the entourage along the bank of a tiny brook feeding into the lake. They were almost at the shore when Malvine shrieked again. "Oh, my goodness," she all but exploded. "Can you believe it? A Peregrine

Falcon, for sure!" The indefatigable busybody aimed her camera into a scraggly cedar that bent far out over the water. "Endangered? Well, I should say."

"Common crow," Highman huffed, obviously tired of Mal's fake discoveries. "*Corvus brachyrhynchos*." The general guffawing that erupted in both groups stopped only when Highman raised her hand to announce further conclusions. "This place is plenty wet," she declared, swatting at a cloud of black flies swarming around her head, "but it most definitely is *not* a wetland."

Her proclamation didn't surprise anybody, and Harry gave Nibber a discouraged look as they began retracing their steps along the brook. Of course it wasn't a wetland. Nothing, not even Mal's persistent search for protected birds, was going to change the outcome of this little expedition. The thin lady had sung. It was over.

The assembly kept quietly to themselves during the retreat, the only sound coming from boots sucking out of the mud. It was hard going, and they stopped for a moment to rest in an open space where the sun kept the flies away. Winston, who had been well behaved all morning, suddenly bolted off to the edge of the brook. Harry called him back, but the dog paid no attention. He was fixed on something, and he didn't stop until he came to a flat rock in the middle of the brook, where he crouched down and uttered a single, low "woof."

Both groups, Highman in front, sloshed off toward the dog, where they saw that the object of his attention was a small turtle, no more than a few inches round. Winston was in a crouch, tail wagging, his rear end in the air and his head down, inches from the tiny creature that had drawn every appendage inside his shell.

Highman shooed Winston and bent down to have a look. After a second or two, she stood up again. "I just don't believe it," she gasped. "I'm pretty sure this is a Spotted Turtle." She reached back down and gently picked up the creature, cupping the shell between her fingers. "I present you *Clemmys guttata*," she said proudly, holding it out for all to see. "In all my time in this part of Maine, I've never seen one." She went on to explain that the uncommon species could sometimes be found in the southern part of the state, but never this far north. In any case, she said, it was a protected species.

Malvine whooped and snapped a dozen pictures. Harry bent in for a closer look, and the turtle stuck its head out and looked back. It was covered in bright yellow polka-dots, all over its dark shell and on its head and tail as well.

Nibber was unable to contain his excitement. "And there's another one," he said, gesturing wildly toward the other side of the narrow brook.

"Leave it!" Highman barked before anybody could move. "It's mating season, and I only need one." She pulled a gunnysack from her knapsack, wet it in the stream, and gently deposited the turtle.

"Well now," she said, pointing to the bag, "this little discovery puts a whole new light on the entire matter. We're going to have to take a pause while the department decides the best way to proceed."

Ted Rafferty hadn't said a word all morning, letting his tightly pinched puss convey his feelings of disdain for the entire expedition, but now he rose up, got directly in Highman's face, and glared down his short nose. "Exactly how much time will this take?" he demanded.

Highman was his match. "As long as necessary," she shot back. "Maybe a week, maybe more. We don't rush into these kinds of things."

Nibber jabbed Harry in the ribs, and they both grinned ear to ear. Within another week, the sales agreement with Fritz Grunwald would be null and void.

*****

Nibber elbowed Harry out of the way, and he and Winston burst into the house. "We won!" he shouted, as giddy as a Little Leaguer home from a game. "Came from behind in the last inning."

Diane waited for Harry to appear and looked at him quizzically. "It's true," Harry said proudly. "Saved by a protected species." He went on to explain that the DEP permitting process had been delayed "all because we found a little Spotted Turtle."

Winston shoved Nibber's leg with his head. "*Winston* found the little Spotted Turtle," Nibber amended.

Diane was curious about the turtle, and Harry filled in the details. As he began to describe the bright yellow dots, a faint light began to glow in his head. "Canary yellow," he specified before turning to look at Nibber, who was holding his sides, laughing out loud.

Harry paused only a second, and the light shone even brighter. He moved to within an inch of his friend's face. "Nibberrrrrr?" He drew out both the name and a confession at the same time.

"I cannot tell a lie," Nibber said, still roaring.

"The lawn chairs! The window box! The front door!" The words tumbled out of Harry's mouth. "All canary yellow."

"The situation called for extreme measures," Nibber explained. "We knew perfectly well there was going to be no winter deer yard," he said, "and we weren't able to flood the place. It was the last resort."

Harry demanded details. "Simple," Nibber said. "You know how those cans of spray paint work. When you get to the very end, they begin to spit little dots of paint. That's the part I needed. Had to use up three cans on other things just to get to the bottoms."

"Yes," Harry remembered, "but I thought you went looking for frogs?"

"I did, but it didn't work," Nibber shrugged. "I was going to make me one or two of a few of those Blue Dart frogs. Got a bunch of Spring Peepers and tried to dye them blue." He squirreled up his face. "Did you know frogs don't take very well to dye?" He didn't wait for an answer. "I held a couple of them by their little arms and dunked them in a jar of blue dye. The color slid right off."

"That wouldn't have fooled anyone, in any case," Diane offered.

"Why not?"

"Blue Darts are found only in Brazil."

"Oh well, the turtles worked much better, anyway."

Harry was dazzled. "Where'd you learn all this stuff?"

"*National Geographic.*"

"You forgot," Diane said. "Nibber reads *National Geographic.*"

"He doesn't read them, he just looks at the pictures," Harry corrected. "He's always loved the pictures."

Nibber went on to regale Diane with the details of painting and planting the turtles. He'd given several of their shells a blue-black base coat, then spotted them with the yellow. "Some didn't come out very good," he said, explaining that he'd let the bad examples go in back of the cabin. The rest, a half-dozen or so, he took to the brook at Fritz's place. His only worry was that nobody would find one during the inspection, and so he'd done some training with Winston by hiding the turtles and giving the dog a treat when he found one.

Harry was half listening, and he stared out the window. Nibber noticed. "Whatsa matter, Harry?" he asked. "Cat got your tongue?"

"I'll tell you exactly what's the matter," Harry said. "Your tinkering with those turtles has done nothin' but put us in a fix. If they were real, there's a chance the DEP would not allow a parking lot anywhere near the place. But they're not real, and pretty soon they're gonna figure it out. Sure, we might get beyond the deadline of the sales agreement, but you already know Fritz is afraid to sell his place to anybody but that snot Rafferty and his gangster buddies. All you've done is make it easier on that crowd by not having to deal with Molony's messy estate." Harry shook his head sadly. "When them chickens come home to roost, our goose is cooked."

Diane seemed pleased with all of the barnyard expressions, mixed up or not. "You really shouldn't look a gift horse in the mouth." She wagged her finger playfully. "Honestly Harry, sometimes you're as stubborn as a mule."

11

Picture Perfect

Nibber came for breakfast and wound up cooking it for himself. Diane pulled a chair a foot or so back from the table, ever so slowly sat down, and stared in dismay at the vast amount of cookware needed to prepare bacon and eggs. "I'll clean up while you and Harry eat," she announced defensively, watching as a sea of grease crept over the stovetop and up the back, "or else the havoc will surely spread."

Harry was focused on Nibber's cooking. "Turn 'em," he said of the eggs, "and let's get a move on." Having worked extra shifts at the mill last week, he had a rare Monday off and was anxious to make the most of it.

Diane's hand roamed over her swollen belly. "I guess I won't be going anywhere," she said ruefully, "except maybe to the funeral on Saturday."

Her comment drew blank looks. "What funeral?" Harry asked.

"Oh, I forgot to tell you," she went on, "Mal Grandbush called to say the good Reverend Peppard has picked Saturday for Jeff Molony's service. The Rebekahs are having a rummage sale on the lawn of Falling Waters that morning, and Peppard thought having the two together might improve the funeral crowd."

Nibber turned to look at Harry. "You goin'?"

Diane didn't wait. "Yes, *both* of you are going. No matter what you two thought of Molony, it's the right thing to do. And I'm going, too, if the baby doesn't come first."

"Oh, I wouldn't worry at all about that," Nibber said. "Primips are often very late."

"Primips?" Harry was puzzled. "We don't know what kind of a baby we're getting yet, and if that's your idea of a name, it's just terrible."

"Of course, you wouldn't understand," Nibber cooed in a condescending sort of way. "It's the medical term for a woman's first baby."

Harry jabbed his egg with a fork, and the yolk rose up onto his hand. "You know," he sputtered, "sometimes it's really hard to figure out why you haven't got full time work."

"Speaking of work," Nibber said, "what sort of jobs are we going to do today, and where will we be if Diane needs me?"

"If Diane needs *us*," Harry said, "we'll begin at the library, to have a look at Malvine's historical photo albums, and then over to Town Hall next door, to examine the documents having to do with the Pond Park venture. "After all that," he said, "if there's time, we really should go to the Watford hoosegow and look in on poor old Horatio Perkins."

*****

The new library had been open since December, but Harry hadn't been there. He intended to wait and have his first look at the dedication ceremony, which he expected might come when the place opened, but Malvine had talked the trustees into putting it off until the summer people arrived when there was a chance for bigger donations. Now, as the time went by without a look-see, he was beginning to feel a little sheepish.

Located in a renovated barn on the road above the dam, the new facility was made possible by an arrangement with Debbie, who had turned the family homestead over to the town shortly before she moved in with Nibber. The main house became the new town offices, and the big barn across the driveway was transformed into a much needed, expanded library.

143

Malvine was standing by the circulation desk when they came in, and her face lit up when she saw Harry. "Well, lookie here," she said, her voice dripping sarcasm. "Harry Crockett! And in the library, of all places."

Harry ignored the comment. "I'm here to have a look at your Belfry history albums," he announced.

In an instant, Malvine turned sticky sweet. "Goodness me," she said, patting Harry on the back. "I'll show you the way." She took his elbow and led him to a reading table near a window where several albums were neatly arranged between a set of carved loon bookends. Spread out on the other end of the table was an array of photographs and clippings not yet catalogued. "That book's going to be called *Pond Park and Another Murder*," she said, nodding proudly at the pile, "but neither of these things is quite yet finished."

Nibber had sauntered off to the magazine section, and Harry sat down to survey the typed labels on the three completed books. The first was from last September, soon after Malvine appointed herself town historian. It was marked *Hurricane Clara*, with a subtitle that read *The Murder of Doc O'Neil*. Harry knew plenty about both of these things, and he passed it over. The next was titled *Christmas Stroll*. He flipped it open for a quick look.

The annual stroll was the Belfry Business Group's final promotional event before the shops were closed and shuttered for the winter. The fire department hung wreaths on telephone poles, and lights were strung above doorways and along the railings over the bridge. John Knight played Santa Claus, giving away roasted chestnuts and hot chocolate in front of the store. Caleb Barnes brought his team of Percherons and gave hayrides from the Sunrise to the bridge and back, where the sidewalks were illuminated with candles placed in brightly colored paper bags.

Harry was anxious to see if Malvine had captured the high point of last December's stroll when one of the bags caught fire and raced up the creosoted wooden post of Will Colchester's mailbox. Sure enough, on the final page of the album was a fine picture of Will, posed next to his charred box and standing with several of his smiling volunteers who had been called out to douse the flames.

Finally, Harry picked up the scrapbook titled *The Burning of the Belfry Grand Hotel*. In front were news clips from the *Watford Journal* along with a multi-page narrative in the historian's own hand. Harry flipped quickly to the pages of photographs she had taken the night of the fire.

Nibber returned from the magazines and sidled up next to Malvine, who had been leaning over Harry's shoulder all along. Harry looked up at her and observed that many of the photographs were either under-exposed or out of focus, or both. "You ought to take the bad ones out," he said, pointing to the very first picture, a black rectangle with two white dots near the center. "Some of these shots are completely worthless."

Malvine bristled. "Historians don't take *anything* out of the record," she scolded. "They keep *everything* and let somebody else be the judge of what's important and what's not."

"So," Harry said, keeping his finger on the first photo, "what could possibly be important about this one?"

"Naturally, they're all in sequence," Malvine explained. "I was the first to arrive on the fire scene, and this one was taken through the car window, on the road leading up to The Grand."

"You got there even *before* Belfry Rescue?" Nibber was astonished.

"Yup, I did. Let me tell you, a police scanner is a most useful tool for a local historian. I keep mine on the kitchen counter, right up next to my log book and the telephone."

"Seems to me you've got your very own dispatch center," Nibber observed. "Sure helps to explain the rapid spread of news around these parts."

The conversation had strayed, and Harry tried to regroup. He again put his finger on the black picture. "So tell me, exactly what are we looking at here."

"As I was about to say," Malvine said, "I turned off the main highway and headed up the road to the hotel. I could see the fire through the windows, and I stopped to take a shot." She pointed to the top of the photo, and for the first time Harry could make out the vague outline of the giant white building against the dark sky. And, sure enough, there was a hint of reddish yellow in the places where the windows would have been.

"I wanted to shoot some more," Malvine went on, "but Will Colchester and his volunteers were right behind me in the rescue truck, yelling and making the siren scream. As if that wasn't distracting enough, at that very moment this car comes barreling toward me from the direction of the hotel."

"The two white dots," Harry filled in. "Headlights." He examined the picture even more closely. "Who was in the car, do you know?"

"I have no idea. I just pulled over to the side to let the rescue truck go by, and as soon as it did the car raced down toward the main road. I didn't recognize the car and couldn't see who it was."

"Would you mind terribly if I borrowed this picture?" Harry asked.

"Take it out of the library, you mean? Like a book?" She thought for a second or two. "Well, I suppose you could. Don't know why not, except you don't have a library card." She thought some more. "Maybe Nibber could take it out on his," she suggested. "He's a library member, at least. Comes here every time *National Geographic* comes out."

"I know," Harry nodded agreeably. "He likes the pictures."

Malvine took Nibber's card, stamped the due date on it and on the back of the photo, and slid the picture into a plastic sandwich bag before ceremoniously presenting it to Nibber who, once they were outside, handed it off to Harry. "Take very good care of this," he said. "I'm responsible." They had gone only a few steps when he piped up again "Why on earth do you want the lousy picture in the first place?"

Harry grinned. "Didn't dare say anything in front of the chief village gossip," he said, "but there's something mighty interesting about this photograph. He took it out of the bag and held it up in the sunlight. "If you look close," he continued, "you can actually see a license plate on that car." He pointed near the middle of the photo to a rectangular hint of green between the twin dots of the headlights. "Not a Maine plate. Maine plates are white, but it's a plate, just the same."

"And?" Nibber was trying to connect the dots.

"Course, we can't make out the number," Harry said, "but I'll bet there's somebody who can."

*****

It was a short walk across the driveway to the new town hall. When they arrived, Harry was surprised to see that the waiting area in front of the service desk was jammed with a number of grumbling, grim-faced people, each one holding what appeared to be a letter. Not one of them was in a hurry, and they readily made way for Harry and Nibber to move up front.

Town manager Susan Hanson spotted the pair and walked briskly out of her office in the back. "And, what can we do for you today?" she asked, all smiles, nice as pie. Harry was pleased to note she was in good humor.

Never mind the irritation of the waiting crowd of cranky citizens, he and Hanson hadn't spoken since the Battle of the Bridge, when it first became clear they were on opposite sides of the Pond Park debate. On that matter, Harry wanted peace and quiet; she wanted property taxes.

Harry leaned over the counter and whispered. "Who's that?" He tossed his head, motioning to the group behind him.

"Tree Committee," she whispered back.

Harry turned abruptly, did some counting, and then turned back. "Seven people? For a Tree Committee?"

Hanson shrugged. "We have lots of trees."

Nibber was interested. "Why are they all here?"

"I think they're waiting for a photographer," she said. "They want to resign as a group."

"Why?"

"I believe one of the selectmen called them a bunch of tree-huggers."

"Is that a *bad* thing?" Nibber wanted to know.

"Maybe it is if you are one."

Harry put things back on track and explained he'd like to see the town papers related to the Pond Park project. He was prepared to make the point that they were public documents, but there was no need. "Of course," Hanson said sweetly as she led them into a back room, "and isn't it wonderful that this terrible, town-splitting controversy is nearly over?"

"Nearly over?" Harry didn't get it.

Susan was matter-of-fact. "Phoebe Highman called from Augusta this morning to say the turtle she found during the DEP inspection was bogus. It's not a Spotted Turtle. It's a common Painted Turtle that somebody made over."

"Bogus?" Nibber exclaimed. "Why on earth do you suppose anybody would do a dumb thing like that?"

"Or, even think they could get away with it." Harry glared at Nibber.

"That's simple," Hanson said. "The opponents wanted the DEP to find some rare species so they'd deny a permit and put an end to Pond Park." She grinned. "I guess the joke's on them."

Harry did some quick figuring. The sales agreement was due to expire on Friday. Five more days. "So, what happens next?"

"You know the State of Maine," Hanson shrugged, "quick as a rabbit with turtles and slow as turtles with paper work. Maybe late this week, Phoebe said, or more likely, early next."

"Early next would be good," Harry said.

Hanson went to a row of filing cabinets in the back of the room and returned with a bulging folder. "It's all here," she said. "Everything we have on Pond Park. Take your time. The permits have been approved, but can't be issued until the DEP signs off and they can't sign off until Lake Land Creations has the deed for the Grunwald property in their hands. Only a matter of days."

Harry began flipping through the papers. There were applications and approvals for all sorts of code requirements – building, fire, electrical, plumbing, even tree protection and signs. The file also included a copy of last winter's transfer of the deed for Gabe Brumbley's property to Lake Land Creations. Harry recalled that Jeff Molony had talked Brumbley into selling without explaining it was to become part of Pond Park. Brumbley felt cheated, and he'd been sore about it ever since. Harry examined the deed closely, then turned to Hanson. "This here deed is signed by somebody," he said, "but it's not Molony."

"Oh, no," Hanson replied. "That would be Ned Rafferty. He signs all the papers for LLC, LLC. He's the president, and he has the authority. The town clerk checked. It's all in order."

"Hard to read his signature," Harry observed. "It's smudged on 'most all of these documents."

"Oh, he drags his hand through the ink," Hanson explained, "but that's his signature all right. I witnessed just about every one of 'em."

Nibber was impatient. "You seen enough?" he asked without knowing what Harry was looking for in the first place.

Harry waited just a bit. "Yes, I think I have seen enough," he said finally, returning the papers to the folder and handing it back to the town manager before he and Nibber headed out the door.

They had no more than stepped outside when they ran square into the hefty deputy sheriff, Kelly Hallowell. Harry was delighted. "Just the person I wanted to see," he declared. Kelly didn't seem at all delighted. "What are you up to?" Harry asked.

"I'm serving papers for just about everybody that's too afraid to deliver 'em for themselves," she said. "I've got court summonses, eviction notices, arrest warrants and now, since Town Meeting, property seizure notices from Belfry. Trust me, a sheriff's life is not an easy one."

"Seems simple enough to me," Nibber jumped in. "Knock on the door, hand over the papers, and run."

"It's the dirty looks," Kelly said. "And, you can be sure when the sheriff knocks at the door, nobody offers refreshments."

"Now, right there's a fine benefit of the job," Nibber laughed, jabbing Kelly in her large belly, prompting her to jab him back before the two of them began shadow boxing around the parking lot.

Harry broke it up. "There's enough," he said, turning to Kelly, who was straightening up her jacket. "How'd you like to do a bit of *real* police work?" he asked. Her eyes lit up. "If you get this right," he said, "you might just become Cebennek County Sheriff of the Year."

"You said that once last fall," Kelly came back, "and I didn't get diddly."

Harry took Malvine's photo out of his pocket. "Look here," he said, tilting it into the light. "It's a picture taken at the beginning of the fire at The Grand. If my hunch is right, it might very well point us to an arsonist. All's we've got to do is get a reading off the license plate right here." He pointed between the two white dots. "I'm sure you know somebody in the crime lab in Augusta who'd be able to figure it out."

Kelly looked doubtful. "Not to worry," Harry said. "It's solid stuff. The photo is marked and dated, and I've got you a most eager witness."

Kelly shrugged, took the photo and was set to leave. "Hold on." Harry reached into the front seat of Nibber's pickup. "There's one other thing, and I think it has to do with the fire, too." He handed Kelly the cardboard box Nibber had been using for electrical supplies. "Maybe you could ask your detective friend to find out where this box came from and what was in it."

Kelly took the box, cocked her head. "As far as I can tell," she said, "I'm still nothin' more than a delivery person."

Harry patted her on the back, then looked at his watch. "Gotta go," he said. "We can be in Watford by noon and look in on the prisoner – if they'll let us."

*****

They stood by the glass enclosure and waited for the desk sergeant to get off the phone. Harry smiled warmly, doing his best to act sure of himself. "We'd like to see the prisoner, Horatio Perkins," he announced.

"Family?"

"Has no family, so far as we know. We're friends."

"Highly irregular," the officer said. "I'll have to check."

155

"Tell the person you check with that we're representing Mr. Perkins," Nibber said, imitating authority.

"Lawyers?"

"Nope," Nibber said. "More important than that. We're defense specialists."

The sergeant looked confused. "Oh, well. Five minutes. That's it." He then led the way down a narrow corridor and through a locked metal door into the brick annex of the Watford Police Department that served as the county jail. He pointed to a small conference room on the left. The door was open and they could see only a well-worn folding table surrounded by four rickety metal chairs. "Wait here," he said.

Harry tested his chair with his hand before he sat down. Nibber didn't sit down at all. It was only a minute before the officer returned, Horatio in tow, wearing handcuffs in front. The officer helped the prisoner into a chair and left the room, closing the door behind him.

Horatio smiled, but only a bit. Harry said the first thing that came into his head. "Have you met with Tony Pasquale?" Horatio brought his cuffed hands up to one ear and leaned in, unsure of what he'd heard. Harry repeated.

"Yes, I did," Horatio finally responded.

"How'd you make out?"

"Take-out?" The veins popped on Horatio's temples. "Why the hell would I want take-out? That's all I ever get in here."

Harry could tell right off that it was going to be a hard session. "HOW DID YOU <u>MAKE</u> <u>OUT</u> WITH PASQUALE?" He leaned into Horatio's face and mouthed each word slowly and carefully.

The mostly deaf man caught it, and he began to explain. "Made out fine," he said. "I told him everything. I really don't know why I'm here. I didn't do anything. I couldn't have killed Molony even if I'd wanted to," he said, and then added, "which I did."

Harry was interested in why Horatio thought he couldn't have done it. All the evidence pointed the other way. "WHY DO YOU SAY YOU COULDN'T HAVE DONE IT? Harry asked the question twice before Horatio understood.

Horatio scratched a nose itch with both hands and began. "That Saturday afternoon at the bridge, when Molony accused me of being a Democrat?" Harry nodded. "I took a swipe at him with my poke oar, and when I missed, I hurt my shoulder. The next afternoon I went to

Knight's Store. Allie Knight knew I was in pain, and she told me I should go to the hospital in Watford and see about it. About three o'clock, I did."

"What time did you leave to come home?" Nibber leaned in from behind a chair.

"That's the problem," Horatio said. "I don't remember, exactly. Pasquale's checking the emergency room records. But, there's a good reason why I can't remember. They gave me some pills, pain killers, and told me not to take any until I got home." He stopped again, as if still trying to remember. "Anyway, it hurt so bad I stopped at the water cooler on the way out of the hospital and popped a couple." His eyes glossed over, even at the thought. "I gotta tell you," he said, "I barely made it home. Went right into bed. Didn't wake up 'til about ten Monday morning. In the meantime, stupid Molony got hisself murdered. It warn't me, that's for sure."

The officer stuck his head around the door. "Time's up." His tone left no room for negotiation.

Harry reached over the table and patted Horatio's bound hands. "Now, don't you worry," he said, trying not to show his own doubts. "Somehow, we'll get you out of this mess."

"Dress?" Horatio looked down at his orange prison garb, perplexed. "I'm not wearing a dress."

12

A Funeral and a Rummage Sale

Despite dark clouds rolling in overhead, Saturday morning's rummage sale at Falling Waters drew the predictably healthy crowd of faithful locals as well as a fair number of early-arriving summer people. Very few had even the slightest idea they were about to help celebrate the life of Jeff Molony.

"Nice day for a funeral," Nibber quipped as he and Harry helped guide Diane over the wet and bumpy lawn.

Debbie was in front, clearing a path. "Pastor Peppard was right," she turned to say. "Having the Rebekahs' sale and the service at the same time was a stroke of genius."

The four nodded greetings here and there and looked carefully as they walked by the row of card tables, groaning with heaps of used clothing, homemade decorations, unusable kitchen gadgets, and unwanted Christmas presents, some still with tags. Diane had just begun to paw through a tangle of baby clothes when the heavens opened up and it began to pour. The organizing ladies moved quickly to pull a tarp over the tables, and the customers had already begun to scurry for cover when the Rev. Peppard appeared on the church steps, his flowing robes nearly filling the full expanse of the double front doors.

"Oh, please," he shouted over the pelting rain, "come inside until the storm passes. It will be dry, I promise."

"It'll be dry, for sure." Nibber spoke in a too-loud voice. "Wait 'til they hear the man preach."

"Shush!" Diane wagged her finger and looked to see if Peppard had overheard. He hadn't. He was too busy luring victims into his trap.

First through the doors was Lorry Devine, closely followed by several other paid mourners, all wearing floppy black hats and clutching tiny purses with embroidered hankies peeking over the tops. Peppard greeted each one with a warm handshake, using the moment to secretly pass along small, white envelopes.

Harry picked out a pew on the left, away from the piano, and the four settled in to examine the proceedings. Lorry and the Sob Sisters filed one by one into a pew at the front, close to the pulpit. The next few rows were filled with church regulars, including Allie and John Knight and several of their uncountable kids. Poor Henry McLaughlin sat across the aisle with his adopted guardians, Trooper Aidan Brown and Deputy Kelly.

The widow Molony had kept her word and was nowhere to be seen. Ned Rafferty, the closest to being family, sat alone, halfway on the right. Molony's partner in the Pond Park scheme held his nose in the air, looking at nobody. In the far back, both sides were sprinkled with a dozen or so flatlanders, now beginning to look a bit doubtful but still grateful to be out of the wet.

Peppard had kept his word to the widow, as well. The principal guest had been properly cremated and was sitting on the altar in a green ceramic urn, painted with what appeared to be tiny images of houses. Nibber noticed the drawings. "I'd guess they represent all the places Bolony got from Belfry foreclosures," he whispered.

This time it was Debbie who touched a finger to her lips. "Shush!"

Peppard had disappeared into the vestry, but at the stroke of ten he returned with an appropriately somber face and a simple black robe. His customary loon-embroidered stole had been replaced with one featuring an application of white flannel doves, and he smoothed the birds carefully over his broad belly as he strode to the lectern.

"We gather here this morning to honor the life of Jeffrey Molony," he began for the benefit of the snared tourists, "a deacon of this church and a force of mighty change in our tiny community."

"I'll say." Nibber whispered again.

"Shush!"

The pastor promptly nodded toward the wizened pianist, Thelma McCracken, who crouched almost eye level with the keyboard as she haltingly plunked out the opening hymn. Although the words were printed on handouts left in the pews, the song was not familiar, and all along the pews, people soundlessly moved their mouths:

And must I be to judgment brought,
And answer in that day
For every vain and idle thought,
And every word I say?
Yes, every secret of my heart
Shall shortly be made known,
And I receive my just desert,
For all that I have done.

As the service wore on, it became apparent that Peppard had gone to some length to personalize the selections. His scripture readings leaned heavily on

Leviticus, a book that describes a wide variety of sins and offers scant options for redemption. Harry was especially taken by the Lord's words to Moses about the sins of deceiving neighbors through robbery and the claim that such thefts "require full compensation, plus a fifth."

"A fifth of what?" Nibber asked into Harry's ear.

"Oh, I donno. *Maker's Mark*, maybe?"

"Shush!"

With very little audience involvement and only brief moments for reflection, the service moved along smoothly and, except for the entertainment of the Sob Sisters weeping on cue, the proceedings were altogether unremarkable until Peppard began what turned out to be a very lengthy homily. As he droned on and on, a few of the flatlanders considered their options and elected to go back out into the rain.

Peppard knew he was losing, and he stepped up his delivery, raising both his voice and his arms in the peroration. In a final dramatic wave, the billowing sleeve of his black robe caught the cremation urn and it began to wobble. The scene unfolded as if in slow motion. Dumfounded, the pastor froze in place. "Dear Jesus," he muttered as the jar made one entire revolution before toppling down on the altar, spilling a teaspoon or two of Molony across the top.

For several seconds, the only sound was the steady pounding of rain on the roof. When Peppard at last recovered, he used the palm of his hand to brush Molony back in the bottle. When he'd gotten all he could, restored the urn to its upright position and wiped his hand on his black robe, leaving a dramatic grey swash down the front. The episode had clearly unsettled him, and he offered an abbreviated and unusually meek benediction before turning to the shrinking pianist for the recessional.

Come, ye sinners, poor and wretched,
Weak and wounded, sick and sore ...

Thelma pecked at the notes and sang at the top of her lungs. A few of Lorry's ladies hummed along, but otherwise, Thelma was on her own and growing ever more disgusted. She stopped abruptly at the end of the first verse and refused to carry on. Peppard hadn't been given time to leave the pulpit, and he leaned into the microphone to announce that the celebration would continue with refreshments in the vestry. Working in unison for the first time, the entire assembly quickly scrambled for the exits. About half of them headed for the front door. The rest trailed Peppard into the small back room, regularly used for Sunday school and church meetings.

Harry edged in front of Peppard, found a comfortable stuffed chair in the corner of the room for Diane, and pulled three folding chairs and a card table up close. "No shortage of sin reminders in here," Nibber observed, pointing around the walls, covered with finger paintings from the children's last lesson, depicting Moses in various stances, carrying stone tablets carefully inscribed with the commandments.

Peppard stayed just inside the door, greeting each guest with apologies for spilling Molony and assuring everybody the guest of honor was now in the safe care of cemetery sexton Digger Hanson, who had placed the urn far back on the Bible table and was stiffly standing guard. The paid mourners, faithful to the end, were milling about, offering strained words of consolation to each other.

"Be right back," Harry said as he and Nibber headed for the refreshment table where the Rebekah ladies had set out the usual fare. They passed by the platter of carrot sticks and celery, and each reached for a cookie in a tray with a penciled label that promised no glucose, cholesterol, sugar or nuts.

"Cardboard," Nibber sputtered after his first nibble.

Henry McLaughlin was in charge of the punch bowl, and he wobbled a bit as he ladled out a paper cupful of the green mixture for Nibber, who took one gulp and made a face. Harry carefully took a sip of his own, grimaced, and glanced down into the wastepaper basket under the table. There, in a fast-growing collection of empty cups, was an empty bottle of *Grey Goose*. Poor Henry had spiked the punch.

Harry wanted to be sure Henry knew he had been discovered. "I'd say you went all out on this one," Harry said, pointing to the bottle.

"Nothing but the best for Molony." Henry had a twinkle in his watery eyes. "But please don't tell the pastor. He's already been 'round for seconds."

Back in the corner, Harry presented Diane a celery stick and a cup of water, and then put several extra cups of punch on the table, well out of her reach. Nibber snagged one, and sat back. "I'm exhausted," he said to no one in particular.

"What on earth for?" Harry wanted to know. "It's been raining. You haven't done a lick of work for days."

"Up all night," Nibber explained, "finished my taxes. Mailed 'em this mornin', right on time. I'm in line for a nice little refund, by the way. Not much reportable income and lots of charitable contributions."

"I hate to be the one to tell you this," Harry said, "but the IRS considers cash payments reportable income."

"Maybe so," Nibber admitted, "but who can keep track of all that stuff?"

Harry moved on. "Anyway, I wasn't talking about this being tax day. Does anybody remember why this particular day is extra special?" Nobody guessed. "Fritz Grunwald's sales agreement expired yesterday, and this is the first day that his property is on the open market, that's what."

Diane squirmed in her padded seat. "Nobody's forgotten that," she said. "It's just that the deadline doesn't really mean much. If what you guys say is true, the old man is so terrorized by Rafferty and the Nurse that he won't be selling his place to anybody but that gangster bunch, in any case."

Harry couldn't help but agree. "Worse than that," he added, "the EPA is just about to issue the permit. That'll likely clinch it for the bad guys."

Nibber threw up his hands in desperation. "Honestly, whenever anybody around here sees a light, you guys run as fast as you can to blow it out." He turned to Harry. "Why don't you go get yourself some more punch? Your cup is half empty." He laughed at his own joke.

Harry couldn't help but grin as well. "Of course, we'll keep trying to work something out," he said, "but you've got to admit, for a long time around here almost everything has a way of going south. First, the Belfry Grand burns to the ground. Then a Boston mob decides to build a permanent carnival smack in the middle of the village. And, as if all of that wasn't enough, we have ourselves another murder." He paused. "Oh yes, and then they put the wrong guy in jail."

His litany of misfortune brought on a moment of reflection, unbroken until Nibber looked around to make sure no one was listening, and then spoke up. "Let me tell you," he said with an air of certainty, "I didn't paint all them gawd-damn turtles for nothin'. You guys can do what you want, but I'm stickin' with the plan. Now, we've got Tony Pasquale on board, and I'm sure he'll find some way to grab that hunk of land right out from under those thugs."

Diane seemed confused. "I thought Pasquale was hired to help Horatio Perkins, not the anti-Pond Park people."

"He said he could help with both things," Nibber grinned, "plus, he's taking care of my speeding ticket, and all for one fee."

"I'd say he has his hands full," Diane said.

"He does indeed," Nibber agreed. "Yesterday, I took one-hundred-and-fifty grand out of the toilet and gave it to him. If lightning strikes, we've got to be ready."

Harry's eyes bugged out. "You get a receipt?"

"Well, no," Nibber admitted, "but we know where he lives."

Harry groaned. Debbie, who had been looking around the room while the others talked, spoke for the first time. "Talking about mysteries," she said, "if I didn't know better, I'd say these people are drunk. And, believe me, I've been a waitress long enough to know the signs. Folks start to laugh at things that aren't funny, and their volume goes way up." She nodded across the room. Poor Henry was still staffing the near-empty punch bowl. Peppard, his paid mourners, Thelma McCracken and a few others, were standing around, pawing each other, laughing and talking loudly.

"Obviously, time to go," Diane observed, "but, before we do, there's one more mystery I'd like to clear up and it has to do with that stupid cardboard box Nibber was using for his electrical stuff. What's become of that?"

"I gave it to Deputy Kelly," Harry said, "and I haven't got a full report, but Kelly told me yesterday she was able to figure out it came from the Mining Company in Clinton, Ohio. That's something, at least. She says the detectives will find out what was in it, but I have a funny feeling it had something to do with the fire at the Belfry Grand."

"So do I," Diane agreed. "In any case, it sure would be helpful to know who got that package."

Nibber looked at Diane, hunched his shoulders. "I asked Hummer who owned Box 681, but he gave me some blather about postal regulations. Like you said, he wouldn't tell me."

"*As* I said," Diane corrected.

Nibber didn't catch on. "I said you said," he said.

"Not to worry," Harry jumped in. "I already know who got it." Everybody sat up and leaned in, and Harry was set to explain when the room suddenly erupted in loud cheering. Peppard was in front of the punch bowl, madly clapping his hands as the Sob Sisters whirled around him, doing a kind of Mexican Hat Dance and stomping on empty paper cups.

Harry waited for the popping noises to stop. "Winston and I went back to Grunwald's place," he said, "and he sniffed out another one of Nibber's painted turtles. I put it in a box and mailed it to Box 681 in Belfry."

Nibber laughed. "Sort of like the *Godfather*," he said, "except you put in a turtle instead of a horse's head."

"At least the turtle was alive," Harry said before Nibber urged him to move on.

Harry strung it out. "I paid Hummer the extra to get a return receipt, and it came back yesterday."

The Sob Sisters had put out another set of cups, and the popping resumed. Harry raised his voice over the din. "It was signed by Ned Rafferty."

13

LLC, LLC

Nibber roared into the Crockett house soon after eleven o'clock, all wound up and full of himself. Tony Pasquale had called a few minutes before, he said, claiming to have some very important news to report and wanting to meet at the Sunrise for lunch.

"On a Sunday?" Harry was a little surprised. "In the middle of the best spring fishing?"

"Said it couldn't wait."

Winston, sleeping off an especially heavy breakfast, raised his head long enough to listen disapprovingly as Nibber asked Diane a few gynecological questions about her current condition, and then went back to sleep. Harry and Nibber headed out the door.

Bo Chilton had gotten around to the annual spring grading of Shore Road, and Nibber's pickup moved quickly along the newly smoothed gravel. "Maybe the cops have found Jeff Molony's real killer," Harry speculated as they pulled onto the main highway, "and old Horatio's been set free."

Nibber squinted into the sun. "I like it when you think positive," he grinned, looking straight ahead. "Frees me up to be doubtful, and, I gotta say, I'm beginning to think the poor deaf man has just about had it."

Harry worked on re-collecting his darker thoughts until they pulled in at the Sunrise, where it was easy to find a place to park. A few shiny sedans of the church-going crowd had replaced Saturday night's assembly of beaters and pickups, and Nibber was able to pull his Chevy up close to the door where they could see inside. Debbie was there, waiting on Lorry Devine and several Sob Sisters, seated at the big table under the wagon wheel chandelier, sipping cups of tea and seeming to all talk at once. Henry McLaughin was the sole occupant at the long bar, and Harry figured poor Henry must have been there since the 9 o'clock opening bell. In the back, comfortably ensconced in their favorite corner booth, they could make out Tony Pasquale, picking at a bowl of fried onion rings and sporting a grin as big as all outdoors.

The lawyer spotted them the second they walked in the door, and waved them over. Debbie hadn't known they were coming, and she wiggled in excitement as she ran to Nibber, who swept her off the floor with a bear hug and twirled her around a few times before he sat her down and slid into the booth opposite Pasquale. "Coffee all around, and keep 'em filled," he said to Debbie, quickly snagging one of Pasquale's rings and drowning it in salted catsup. "And," he added with a certain air, "it's all on me."

"Keep your orders simple," Debbie warned. "Cook's off and the meatloaf's getting old." They ordered bacon and eggs all around, before Nibber turned to Pasquale.

"What's up? This is all about my speeding ticket, isn't it?"

"Pay him no attention." Harry grabbed a ring of his own.

The lawyer's eyes twinkled. "As a matter of fact, you can forget about that ticket. It's all taken care of. You're no longer a fugitive. Easiest case I've ever had. I said you were prepared to fight on grounds of the Good Samaritan law, and they tore it up."

Nibber was very appreciative. "Gee, thanks," he said, "so, I suppose now you're gonna tell us you've sprung Horatio Perkins from the hoosegow."

Harry groaned. "For God's sake, Nibber, Mr. Pasquale called the meeting. Why don't you let *him* set the agenda?"

Pasquale's fly-fishing vest was unzipped and they could see his belly jiggle when he laughed. "I'm afraid this meeting doesn't have anything to do with the murder.

There's been no news on that front, but I can tell you one thing." He pointed at Harry. "I've come around to agreeing with you. Even though all the evidence points at my client, I honestly don't believe he did it." Harry's face brightened, and the lawyer went on to confess that most of his clients were guilty as sin. At first, he said, he'd thought Horatio was no different from the rest. "When they get caught," he said, "these bad guys suddenly act all sweet and innocent," he said. "Like Mother Theresa."

"Or Willie Sutton," Nibber added helpfully.

"Yeah, well, you know what I mean," Pasquale went on. "But this Perkins guy truly *is* sweet and innocent. A pussycat. A deaf pussycat. A clueless, deaf pussycat." There was a break while they conjured the image. "But," the lawyer continued, "I know it will take more than how the man looks to get him off, and I've got me a start in that direction."

Harry thought he knew what was coming and, sure enough, Pasquale proceeded to explain that he'd gotten Perkins' permission to talk with the doctor in the emergency room at Watford Hospital. "He told me the man had a torn left supraspinatus." He made a face. "Pretty painful stuff, I'd say. The doc gave him a few tabs of oxycodone and told him to wait until he got home before he took it, but, as you already know, Perkins claims his shoulder hurt so bad he took a couple right there at the hospital bubbler. You can be sure he was zonked out by the time he got home, certainly in no shape to manage a boat and use it to commit a murder." He paused, for effect. "I don't know who that wacky librarian saw in the boat that night, but it doesn't seem to me it could have been Horatio Perkins."

With that, Pasquale appeared to rest his case, and Harry began thinking like a prosecutor. "'Course, you can't prove he ever took the pills. No witnesses. Just Horatio's word."

Nibber was several lines behind. "What's a supraspinatus?"

"Rotator cuff," Pasquale explained.

Harry scowled at Nibber. "For a guy who styles himself as an obstetrician, you're really pretty stupid when it comes to orthopedics."

Pasquale roared. "Anyway," he said, "I've got more work to do before Perkins goes to the Grand Jury on Tuesday, but I'm beginning to think we might be able to raise enough doubts to turn this thing around." He wiped his face with a napkin. "'Course, it would help a great deal if somebody could finger the *real* killer."

Nobody said a word, and Pasquale was set to move on to the main item when Nibber raised his hand. "The coffee has fully circulated," he said. "Don't start 'til I get back." He headed off to the unisex bathroom behind the bar, and Harry turned to Pasquale.

"This has nothing whatever to do with his bladder," he explained, at the same time nodding toward Debbie, who was headed their way with the tab. "It's all about his wallet."

Harry paid the bill and promised that Nibber would take care of the tip. When Debbie left, Harry leaned across the table, cupped his hands in front of his mouth. "While we're on the subject," he said in a low voice, "let me give you my take on the murder of Jeff Molony."

The lawyer leaned in and listened intently. His eyes grew wider as Harry explained, finishing just as Nibber came out the restroom door, fumbling with his fly. "Anyway," Harry wound up, "I've given all of this stuff to Deputy Kelly, and I'm sure she's already passed it on. It'll make her look good if I'm right."

Pasquale beamed. "Interesting. Very interesting. Come Tuesday morning, it might make me look good, too," he said.

"What's interesting?" Nibber asked as he sat back down.

Pasquale was quick. "What I'm going to tell you next is what's interesting," he said, reaching into a worn briefcase under his seat, "which is why I brought you here in the first place." He slowly slid a set of papers across the table, careful to cover the writing with his hand. "You will recall I promised to set up a corporation so you could remain anonymous if the time ever came when you could buy the Grunwald property and stop the Pond Park travesty." He said it as a question.

"You mean a TLC?" Nibber took a stab.

Harry rolled his eyes. "An LLC, dummy."

"A limited liability company indeed," Pasquale nodded. "And, I'm pleased to say, it is official." He took his hands away from the papers. "Here it is, all tight and legal. I named myself the president and signed it so's to get things going. We can add other officers later, as you please."

Nibber began to speculate on his own corporate position and suggested the role of chief operating officer, but Harry cut him off. "So, what'd you name it?"

"Lake Land Conservation, LLC."

Harry caught on quickly. "Another LLC, LLC! Is that legal?"

"The mobsters named their corporation Lake Land Creations, and it's in Massachusetts," Pasquale explained. "Ours is Lake Land Conservation, and it's in Maine. Just the letters are the same. Not a problem at all."

"Yeah, but why?" Nibber wanted to know.

"You'll find out in a minute."

Harry's head was spinning. "That's all well and good," he said, "and we thank you for that. But really, don't you think we've done little more than set ourselves up for failure?"

Nibber wasn't buying. "Think about it," he said. "The sales agreement between Grunwald and Molony has expired. We've got ourselves a secret corporation and Mr. Pasquale here has got the money."

"Not that simple." Harry shook his head. "The word around town is that the DEP permit was issued Friday. It's a go for the Pond Parkers, never mind that the sales agreement has expired." Harry was on a downhill roll. "In fact, them not having to deal with Molony's estate makes it a whole lot easier." He let out a long, slow sigh. "We're sunk. Sunk for sure."

Nibber hadn't given up. "We've come this far. It won't hurt a bit to at least try."

Pasquale had been listening to the debate with amusement, and he jumped in. "I've taken that option off the table," he announced with a broad smile. "I went to see Fritz Grunwald this very morning. That's why I called you."

"You did?" Harry and Nibber spoke at once.

"I did."

"What happened?"

Pasquale held up his hands. "I dropped in about eight o'clock," he said. "The man was jittery the second he opened the door, and I did my best to calm him down. I explained that I represented the LLC, LLC and that I'd come to buy his property. I was carrying the two plastic bags of cash, and I held them up and told him what they were."

"What'd he say?"

"Jesus!"

"Figures."

"Now I get it," Nibber jumped in. "The LLC, LLC. Fritz thought you were representing Rafferty and that whole bunch." He squirreled up his face. "Was that honest, do you think?"

"Tell me what I said that wasn't true," the lawyer challenged, cocking his head.

"Well, now that I think about it, I guess there must be a difference between truth and honesty," Harry suggested.

Pasquale didn't budge. "Sometimes, you just have to step up and do what's good for somebody when they don't know what's good for themselves. Besides, Grunwald wouldn't dare do it even if he knew he should."

The train of thought confused Nibber, and he skipped over it. "So, what happened?"

"Well, you see, the old tightwad began counting the cash, right there on the kitchen table. It took him a long time, as you might guess, and I let him be, used the time to look around the place. Nice stuff. From the old country, no doubt."

Harry wasn't interested in antiques. "So, what happened?"

"He made piles. Counted it twice. He claimed I was $20 short of $150,000." Pasquale looked at Nibber. "I put it in."

"And?"

Pasquale reached into his briefcase again. "Right here is the deed to Grunwald's property, made to Lake Land

Conservation, LLC." He grinned from ear to ear. "Pond Park is dead."

Harry and Nibber looked at each other in astonishment. Nobody said a word.

"What's the matter? I thought you guys would be thrilled." Pasquale looked disappointed.

"Oh," Harry apologized, "we are thrilled, of course, but it's just that if Pond Park is dead, old Fritz Grunwald could be, too." He turned to Pasquale. "You call Deputy Kelly," he ordered. "Tell her to meet us at the Grunwald place as fast as she can, and ask her to bring Trooper Aidan Brown with her, if she can find him."

All three jumped up from the booth. Harry and Nibber ran for the door. Pasquale headed for the telephone near the bar. Harry yelled to him. "And, don't you dare come anywhere near that place yourself."

14

The Last Cuckoo

It took only a couple of minutes to drive the short distance from the Sunrise to the Grunwald place, but they knew the instant they pulled into the driveway they were too late. Ned Rafferty's black Hummer was parked up close to the garage, and angry shouts were coming through the open windows of the house.

Harry jumped out of the truck and motioned for Nibber to follow. "We've got to go in there, no matter what," he said. "Fritz is in a peck of trouble."

Nibber didn't seem to think it was such a good idea, and he carefully tiptoed several steps behind. "What on earth will we say when we get in there?" he wanted to know. It was a reasonable question, and Harry was working on a reply when the yelling picked up.

"You damned fool! You've screwed us." It was a man's voice. Not Rafferty's, certainly not Grunwald's. "Don't think for a minute that you're going to get away with this."

Nibber gulped, walked even slower. "The Nurse, you think?"

Harry nodded. "'Fraid so."

The yelling didn't stop until they were interrupted by Harry's raps on the door, making sounds a bit louder than his pounding heart. Nobody seemed to want to answer, and Harry walked straight in. Nibber drew his neck into his shoulders, took a deep breath, and followed.

As his eyes adjusted to the light, Harry could see they were in some kind of a sitting parlor, filled with dark furniture and odd, old pictures. He sidled up next to a tiny desk just inside the door and noticed that Fritz's diary was on the top, opened to April 14. He looked down and could make out the single, scrawled entry: "agreement expires today." Fritz himself was standing in the middle of the room, shaking. The man glanced up briefly, gave Harry a pitiful pleading look, and then resumed staring down at the carpet. Ned Rafferty, leaning up against the dark, flowered wallpaper on the left, didn't look up at all. Instead, his sour puss stayed fixed on a man sitting in a large stuffed chair on the back wall, directly under a large, walnut Cuckoo clock.

Harry broke the awkward silence. "Nice clock," he muttered, at the same time feeling a bit foolish at not knowing what else to say.

"And, who the hell are you?" The growl came from the chair, the same voice they'd heard outside. Heavy-set and almost bald, the man looked to Harry as if he were used to being in charge. He wore a brightly colored shirt, smartly creased tan chinos, and shiny black loafers. An ugly red scar ran for an inch or so above his left eye, making his face seem a bit lop-sided, and his thin lips stretched into a smirk as he moved to the edge of the chair, his beady, black eyes demanding an answer.

"I'm Harry Crockett, and this here is my friend, Nicholai Nabroski. Most people call him Nibber."

The man wasn't interested in nicknames. "And, what tha hell da ya want?"

"We're here to call on our friend Fritz," Nibber piped up, nodding at the motionless man in the middle of the rug. "We come by 'most every Sunday, just to be nice."

"You're lyin'," the man shot back without a pause, "'else you'd already have known about the friggin' clock."

Harry took a deep breath and moved bravely away from Nibber's fib. "And so, who are you?"

"None a ya damned business," the man snapped back, inching farther forward in his chair, "but, since you claim to be such good friends of Mr. Grunwald, maybe you can tell us what you know about the swindling that took place here this morning."

Harry dodged the question and tried to act surprised. "Someone was swindled? Who? How?"

"I got a sneakin' feeling you already know," the man sneered, "but I'll tell you anyway." He pointed at the shaking Grunwald. "This guy had an agreement to sell this place to Jeff Molony, but it has expired."

"So's Molony." Nibber interjected impishly.

The man shot Nibber a withering look, and then continued. "We had ourselves an understanding that Mr. Grunwald would sell his property to us, no matter what, but early this morning a goombah lawyer name of Tony Pasquale walks in and claims to represent our company, Lake Land Creations. He then proceeds to dupe stupid Fritzy here into selling the place to him. Gawd-damn sneaky, if you ask me."

"I can't stand sneaky people." Nibber was nervous, and couldn't keep his mouth shut.

"Me neither," the man said, "but you can be sure that grease ball will get what's coming to him." He drew an index finger along his throat. "In the meantime, we've come up with our own solution to our little problem." He glared at Grunwald and at the same time cracked a fist down hard onto the wooden arm of the chair. "Haven't we, Fritzy?"

Grunwald jumped, and then stared at the wobbling armrest. "Jesus!"

The man turned back to Harry. "You see, the law says a man has twenty-four hours to back out on any sale of property. Doesn't need any reason at all." His head snapped back to the middle. "And, that's exactly what you've decided to do, isn't it, Fritzy?"

Another "Jesus" and a hasty nod.

Harry's mind raced. Nobody had thought about the escape clause. Maybe Pond Park wasn't dead, after all. He glanced over at Rafferty, still looking as if he was part of the flowered wallpaper. No doubt about it, the snot was enjoying the entire show. Harry had just begun to consider how he and Nibber might quietly get away when there came a single, very loud knock on the door. "God almighty," the man in the chair growled, "what in hell are we having here, an open house?"

Nibber had never moved far from the door, and when he reached to pull it open, a broad smile came over his face. It was trooper Aidan Brown, all six-feet-two of him, standing tall, shoulders back, his gray uniform Stetson cradled smartly under his arm.

In an instant, Brown slid past Nibber, mumbled something about Deputy Kelly being some distance away, and went across the carpet to join Grunwald in the center of the room. Nibber flashed a grin at Harry. Rafferty swapped puzzled looks with the man in the chair. Grunwald continued examining the carpet.

"How very fortunate," Brown said as he slowly scanned the faces in the room. "It's not often I run into two people I need to talk to at the same time."

"If it's about the speeding ticket," Nibber interrupted, "the entire thing was a huge mistake, and it's all been taken care of."

Brown shook his head. "This is lots more important than any speeding ticket," he said, pointing his finger at the man in the chair. "If I'm not mistaken, sir, your name's Michael Corrado." He looked down at a tiny photograph he'd pulled from his shirt pocket. "Otherwise known as the Nurse. Am I right?"

The man was not fazed by a uniform. "What's it to you?"

"Means nothing at all to me," Brown replied calmly, "but it's really going to please a couple of detectives who sent me looking for you. I'm actually here on their behalf, to ask a couple of questions."

"About what?" The Nurse had calmed down, but only a bit.

Brown again looked around the room. "Perhaps it would be better if the two of us went out to the cruiser and had our little talk in private."

"I'm not movin' one bloody inch for some backwoods rube cop." The Nurse was again crabby.

Brown wasn't rattled. "Have it your own way," he said. "I can just as well ask the questions right here." He moved directly in front of the chair. "I'd like to talk about last December's fire at the Belfry Grand Hotel."

Nibber gave Harry an astonished look, and Harry smiled and turned to catch a glimpse of Rafferty, whose mouth suddenly took on the shape of an "O." Small beads of perspiration popped up on the man's wide forehead, and his reading glasses slipped from his forehead, saved from falling off completely by the bump and the end of his upturned nose.

The Nurse slowly turned his palms up. "What about the friggin fire?" he asked in cool fashion. "The fire marshal's office said it was an accident. What else is there to know?"

"Well, to begin with," Brown said, "maybe you can tell me about ordering a fire ignition device from the Acme Mining Company in Clinton, Ohio, last November."

Harry thought he heard the Nurse suck in a bit of air, but the man said nothing. Rafferty made a nervous cough. Brown moved on.

"And, did you not rent a car in Boston last December 21 and drive it to Belfry?"

"So what if I did?"

"Okay, fine," Brown shrugged. "I can plainly see this is going nowhere. You don't want to answer, don't answer. I'll just take you down to Augusta and let somebody else get to the bottom of this. Those guys are much better at these kinds of things than I am, anyway."

Brown took one final step toward the chair and was about to grab the man's arm when the Nurse quickly bent down and slid his hand under his pant leg. In a single motion, he pulled out a small, snub-nose revolver and pointed it directly at the trooper's head. "In a pig's ass, you will," he said, steadying the snub-nose with both hands.

Brown knew he had been taken and for a moment, seemed a bit embarrassed. "Now look," he finally said, fixing his eyes on the Nurse, "pulling a gun on an officer is a *much* bigger deal than getting brought in for questioning about some hotel fire. You'd best put that thing down right now, before someone gets hurt."

Nibber and Harry had started to back-pedal to the door, but the Nurse waved his revolver and brought them back. Poor Fritz hadn't moved at all, except now he was shaking violently and muttering an unbroken stream of Jesuses.

The Nurse kept his gun trained on the trooper and looked around the room. "Well now," he said after apparently considering his options, "I guess I'm just gonna have to leave you boys," he smirked. "And, don't even bother to try to find me. I've evaporated plenty of times before." He shot a glance at Rafferty, quavering in the flowers. "You go out to that big-assed Hummer of yours and find me some rope, or maybe some of that duct tape you guys around here love so much."

Rafferty's once-pink face drained of all color as he obediently headed for the door. Harry stared at Nibber, whose eyes were frozen on the pistol. Fritz was down on his knees, pawing away with his hands as if trying to dig a hole.

Harry was calculating the chances of winning a wrestling match with the armed Nurse when all at once the already dim light in the room went down a notch. He turned and fought back a cheer when he saw Deputy Kelly in the doorway, her broad figure blocking the sunlight. She was holding her Glock 45 pistol in front, and she accompanied her surprise entrance with a deep-voiced bark: "DROP IT!"

The stalemate lasted only a second before Kelly's gun went off. KABOOM! The explosion ricocheted back and forth across the tiny room, and everyone instantly raised their hands to their ears except Kelly and the Nurse, who put his hands well past his ears and straight up in the air.

"You gawd damn fat fool," the Nurse yelled, "I give up!" The bullet had missed him by mere inches, striking the Cuckoo clock above his head and making a gaping, smoldering hole in the very center of the dial.

Kelly lowered her pistol ever so slightly. For a second, Harry feared she might be thinking about taking revenge for the insult when everything seemed to happen all at once. The Nurse tossed the snub-nose out of his raised hand and sent it careening across the carpet. Harry made a dive for it, and Brown drew his own piece and jumped forward, stuck the barrel in the Nurse's ribs with one hand and smoothly snapped on handcuffs with the other.

It was over as quickly as it had begun. The room reeked of burnt gunpowder, and the only sound was from the Cuckoo bird that must have lunged frantically out of its hole at the moment of impact and was now lolling upside down at the end of its tether, croaking final good-byes.

Brown yanked the Nurse roughly to his feet. "You're under arrest," he said, "for criminal threatening with a weapon."

Nibber eyed the handcuffs, and his confidence improved. "And, for threatening a police officer, at that," he added. "Guess that would make the arson business seem quite tame."

Brown poked the Nurse toward the door. "Great job, Kelly," he said. "You saved the day."

Nibber pointed at Brown. "And, she saved your butt," he said, back in full form.

The trooper smiled. "I'll be right back," he said, "after I've got him settled in the cruiser."

When they left, Harry sidled up to Deputy Kelly. "Yes," he said as he delicately passed her the Nurse's snub-nose, "it was a really great job." He tapped his ears to stop the ringing. "Sheriff of the Year, no doubt about it."

Kelly absent-mindedly clicked the safety on the snub-nose, shoved it in her pocket, and gawked in wonderment at the still-smoking barrel of her Glock. "Gee whiz," she said, looking up at Harry, "I really didn't mean for the thing to go off." She shook her head, mystified. "Hadn't fired it since the academy. Forgot all about the hair trigger."

Harry chuckled, then whispered. "I'll never tell."

Brown was back in a flash, and resumed his place next to Grunwald, who was intently trying to stuff his dead Cuckoo back in the shattered clock. "I'm not finished here," the trooper announced. "As you may recall, before all hell broke loose I said there were *two* people here that I needed to talk to." He wheeled around to face Ned Rafferty, who seemed to have his mind elsewhere.

"I just don't believe it," Rafferty spoke up for the first time. "The son of a bitch burned down my hotel." Brown gave him a dismissive look, but Rafferty went on in Judas fashion. "When the renovation costs were piling up, he mentioned the idea of burning the place a couple of times, but I never once thought he'd actually do it." He looked around to see if his story was catching. It wasn't. "As you all know, I was out of town at the time of the fire," he said, still trying to build a wall. He slowly wagged his head in mock regret. "If I'd ever known what he had up his sleeve, you can be sure I'd have turned him in."

Brown wasn't being fooled, and he interrupted. "I wouldn't say another word, if I were you," he said, "because the day's fast coming when you are going to have to explain why you took shipment of the device that started the fire in the first place."

Rafferty never flinched. "Oh, that" he said, dismissively. "I can explain all that."

"Save it." Brown put up a hand. "Besides, I'm done talking about arson. I'd much rather talk to you about the murder of Jeff Molony."

Again, Nibber gave Harry an astonished look, and again, Harry couldn't help but grin. *Be damned*, he thought, *Kelly did her homework.*

Rafferty was all of a sudden his old, arrogant self. "What in hell are you talking about?" he demanded. "If you think I had anything to do with the murder of Jeff Molony, you're plain crazy. Horatio Perkins did it. You know that. For God sake, you got the man already in jail."

Brown smiled, shook his head. "You're right about that," he said. "Poor Mr. Perkins actually is in jail at the moment, but tomorrow morning the AG is filing a written petition for the dismissal of all complaints against him. I'm guessing he'll be back home for supper."

199

Rafferty's face turned a bright red, and he began to sputter incoherently. Brown nodded at Kelly, who had been cheerfully dangling her own set of cuffs waiting the chance to clamp them on. "You are under arrest for the murder of Jeff Molony," the trooper said to Rafferty, "and I must tell you that you have the right to remain silent ..."

Brown had no more than finished the full rights of Miranda, when Rafferty promptly chose to ignore them. "You're all complete idiots," he fairly screamed. "You know Molony was my friend. Why would I kill him?"

Deputy Kelly seemed eager to play a role. "Since you ask," she said, "I'll tell you. You killed him because he was going to screw you and the rest of the Pond Park schemers. He schemed to buy the Grunwald property all by himself and then turn around and gouge you for it. When you found out about it, it was curtains for Molony. There's your motive, plain enough."

Brown scowled at Kelly. "Stop," he said. "The state has its case; he'll get the details soon enough." He then yanked Rafferty away from the wallpaper and proceeded to herd him toward the door. Nibber went to comfort Fritz, who had now turned his invocations toward the splintered wooden arm of his heirloom chair. Harry and Kelly went outside and talked quietly with each other as they watched Brown ease Rafferty into the now crowded back seat of the cruiser and drive away. After several minutes, Nibber came outside to join them.

"Quite a day, huh?" Harry nodded to his friend.

"Yes, indeed," Nibber replied, giving Kelly a solid whop on the back. "There's some things I don't quite get, but there's no denying that Belfry has just rung up its first-ever triple play."

"Yup," Kelly said, "Pond Park, an arsonist and a murderer, all tagged out in a single day."

15

Out of Left Field

It was a rare warm day for April in Maine, and everybody was out on the front porch of the Crockett house, hoping to catch a late afternoon breeze coming off the lake. Diane squirmed in the big wooden rocking chair, fidgeting with the folds of her maternity shift that had long been let out to the limit of its strings. Lolling on the floor nearby, Winston panted in the heat while he watched to keep his bushy tail clear of the menacing rockers.

Leaning on the porch rail nearby, Harry sipped his ice-shaken martini and looked on in amusement as Nibber and Debbie playfully wrestled for space on a lounge chair built for one. Harry winked at Diane, who giggled at the sweaty sight of tangled arms and legs. "Good lord," she finally exclaimed, "you two must be *very* hot."

"You got that right," Nibber replied. He knew perfectly well what she meant, and she knew what he meant, as well. They weren't the same thing at all.

"Shush!" Diane scolded as Debbie plucked the lime slice off the top of her Corona bottle and offered Nibber a nibble. "Oh, sweetie," she purred, "you are just tooo funny."

Harry stifled a gag and flicked a fingernail on the rim of his glass, making an echoing ring that prompted everybody, including Winston, to sit straight up. "Why don't we have a little review of the day's events," he offered, "especially for the benefit of those of us who haven't quite yet figured it out."

"That would include me," Nibber admitted. "I get almost all of it, but I still don't understand why the cops think Ned Rafferty knocked off Jeff Molony. I must have missed something."

Harry started to spell it out when Diane cut him short. "That can wait," she said, holding up her hand. "First, we must raise a toast to the end of Pond Park. It's by far the best news of the day; forget about arsonists and murderers." She reached awkwardly to click her iced tea against Harry's martini.

"We have Tony Pasquale to thank for the demise of the theme park," Harry declared, raising his glass to Nibber, who suddenly looked hurt. "And, of course," Harry quickly added, "thanks as well to Nibber, for painting the turtles and buying us some time." At that, the dog issued a disgusted sigh from his place on the floor, and Harry was called to toss another rose. "And, we must not forget Winston, who found the turtles."

Nibber had regained his cheerfulness. He scratched his head. "Now that I think about it," he said, "I'm afraid we have to admit that, after what's happened to Rafferty and the Nurse, Pond Park probably would have sunk without any help at all from us."

Harry disagreed. "Don't forget," he came back. "Mobsters are like starfish. Chop off one or two legs, and they grow 'em right back. Now, at least, we own the place, and nobody's going to turn Belfry into a damned amusement park."

"What you mean to say is that Lake Land Conservation owns the place," Diane said, pausing to consider her own correction. "And, now what do you suppose our fine little LLC, LLC is going to do with it?"

Harry had given the matter some thought, and he sipped his gin as he gazed down the hazy lake. "I think we ought to put the property into some kind of a land trust," he suggested, "maybe with the Tree Committee."

"There's no Tree Committee to give it to," Nibber chuckled. "They all up and quit."

"Whatever," Harry said, shrugging his shoulders. "In any case, we own the property, Pond Park is out of business, and old Fritzy is out of debt."

Nibber nodded. "Yes, and I think we should let him go on living in that same house. He never wanted to move out in the first place, just needed the money. Now, maybe he could pay the DDT a small rent and stay right where he is, happily ever after."

"That would be the LLC," Harry said.

It was Nibber's turn to shrug. "Of course, if Fritz stays put, Horatio Perkins can go right on renting the Grunwald cabin by the stream. He won't have to move, either. He'll love that."

"And," Diane chipped in with a grin, "Malvine Grandbush will be positively thrilled to be able to continue spying on him every day. The poor, deaf man no doubt needs that, too."

Debbie whistled over the top of her Corona. "Golly," she gushed, "this whole thing is ending up just like a fairy tale."

"Pond Park might be a fairy tale," Harry said, "but the story of the Belfry Grand isn't at all."

"Certainly not if you were cheering for the Nurse," Nibber observed.

Harry decided it was a good time to recount the Belfry Grand saga from the top. The renovations were costing too much money, he explained, and Rafferty, the Nurse and their Black Wharf Gang backers decided to burn it down, collect the insurance money, and build a theme park in its place. That much, everybody knew.

"So," Harry explained, "the Nurse goes out and buys himself a fancy, radio-operated igniter and has it mailed to an anonymous post office box that Rafferty set up just for that purpose. Then, they set up alibis for Molony and Rafferty, who were sure to be prime suspects when The Grand burned down. After that, the Nurse rents a car, sneaks into town, and torches the place."

"Good plan, except for one thing," Diane admitted. "He got caught."

"Credit the Belfry historian for that," Harry said. "If it wasn't for Mal's picture-taking the night of the fire, they'd never have been able to prove the Nurse was on the scene when it started." He explained that Deputy Kelly told him at the Grunwald place after the arrests that the state crime lab was able to get the plate number off the dark photograph, trace it to a car rental place in Boston, and confirm Michael Corrado, the Nurse, as the renter.

"That reminds me," Harry said, "I must remember to tell Mal the picture she made me sign out at the library has become state's evidence. It'll be well past the due date before she gets it back. She'll bill me for it, I just know."

Diane began thinking in lawyer fashion. "I don't see how the picture proves anything but the fact that the rental car was here. Doesn't really prove the Nurse was with it."

"Yup, circumstantial evidence," Harry admitted, "but there's actually some honest-to-god proof the Nurse was in Belfry that day." He turned to Nibber. "At Knight's Store the night of the murder, Fritz Grunwald told us he first met Corrado just before Christmas, when the guy came to his house to inquire about buying the property. Fritz is a diary keeper. I saw his book this afternoon, on the desk in the parlor. Kelly's gone back to check, but you can bet she'll find the Nurse visited Grunwald on December 21, the day of the fire."

"Goodness," Diane said, "the poor, nervous man will likely have to testify." All four began to laugh at the image of Grunwald trembling on the witness stand.

"Let's just hope the judge loves Jesus," Nibber said.

"So, that settles that." Debbie seemed briefly unconfused. "And, now we must thank Nibber for providing the rest of the evidence." She patted his knee. "If he hadn't had the clear presence of mind to pick up that mailing box at The Grand, nobody would ever have known how the fire was started."

Harry shook his head. "For the love of Pete, Debbie, he took the box because he needed something to carry his widgets in, that's all."

Nibber jumped back. "I suggest you think about it," he replied. "Without me, there's no box, and without the box, there's no evidence. Cut and dried."

"And, what exactly was that ignition device, anyway?" Diane was still in court.

"Simple enough," Harry said. "Kelly said the manufacturer told the detectives that the thing comes in a cardboard container no bigger than a fist. There's a piece of sodium metal in a container of yellow chlorine gas in the bottom, and on the top there's a tiny vial of plain water." He used his hands to draw the picture. "A radio signal triggers a switch that spills the water into the gas, and *whoosh*, the thing makes a flash big enough to catch the container itself on fire. When the rig is placed on something flammable, like a freshly oiled wooden floor, you've got yourself a dandy fire." He looked around inquiringly. "Haven't you ever thought it was strange that the dining room floor was oiled before the renovation work was done?"

Nibber pretended he'd thought about it. "And, of course the fire consumed the evidence. Whatever tiny bits were left got buried in the foundation, under several feet of ashes. No wonder the fire marshal was stumped."

They sat in silence, digesting the undoing of the mobster arsonist, until Nibber spoke up again. "Okay," he said, looking at Harry. "Let's get on to the good part. Why do you think the snot Ned Rafferty killed Jeff Molony?"

Diane raised a warning finger. "What say we skip over the things we already know? If Rafferty did it, he did it because he found out Molony was going to buy out Grunwald and turn around and sell it to the Pond Parkers for a profit. There's your motive, plain and simple. Move on from there."

Harry wasn't in any hurry. "Nobody thought it was unusual when Molony made the sales agreement," he said. "He'd been a stalking horse for the developers right along. What got overlooked was that Rafferty was always the one who made the final deal on Pond Park business. We learned that when Susan Hanson showed the Pond Park papers at town hall. He'd signed all of 'em."

Nibber nodded knowingly. "There really is no honor among thieves," he pronounced, sage-like. "Bolony was a double-crosser, and they wiped him out. End of story."

"Not the end," Diane said, once again shifting awkwardly in the rocker, "we're still a long way from nailing 'the snot,' as you like to call him."

"Fair enough," Harry agreed. "Beyond the motive, we also have opportunity." He looked again at Nibber. "All we have to do is go back to Knight's on the night the body was discovered. Allie Knight told us that Molony, Rafferty, and Horatio Perkins were all in the store that afternoon. Allie convinced Horatio to go to the hospital and see about his shoulder. Rafferty knew that, and he also had a pretty good idea about how long Horatio would be gone. Molony was there because Allie told us he cut the cash line, explaining he was anxious to get out in his kayak. Rafferty heard that, too."

"So, you see," Nibber said in summation, "Rafferty had plenty of time to go to Grunwald's place, borrow the boat, and bash into Bolony when he paddled out the stream."

"And," Harry added, "he also had time to tow the damaged kayak up into North Bay, hoping the evidence would be lost forever." Nibber waved a hand and made a smirk. "Yes," Harry went on. "Nibber found the kayak while looking for frogs when he really needed turtles."

"I'm not sure how far that gets us," Diane laughed. "Now, you've got to tell us exactly what kind of evidence there is that puts the finger directly on Rafferty."

Harry was clearly enjoying the moment. "Because he's left-handed," he said flatly, letting his blunt answer hang out in the warm spring air.

Nibber didn't go exactly to the point. "Rafferty is left-handed?"

"Easy enough to prove," Harry said, "but we already know it already, anyway. At town hall, I asked Susan why Rafferty's signatures were all smudged. She explained that he drags his hand through the ink. Only left-handers do that."

"So what?" Diane pressed on.

"Because, whoever rammed Molony with the boat that night was left-handed," Harry said. "And, we know that for a couple of reasons. First, when Nibber and I went into Horatio's boathouse after we retrieved the red kayak, we could see where the cushion had been removed from its usual place on the left stern seat and stowed under the right side. Horatio is right-handed and sits on the left to manage the tiller. That's what all right-handers do. "

Nibber, Debbie and Diane were making hand gestures, left and right, trying to keep up with Harry. "That was just a tiny clue, not real evidence," he admitted. "But, here's the clincher." He proceeded to recall the conversation he and Nibber had with Malvine Grandbush that same night, after the cops had gone. "She told us she'd been watching out the window when Perkins headed his boat straight toward her. That would have put the left side of the boat facing the lake. She said he suddenly took a sharp turn inward, toward the head of the stream."

Nobody's lights came on, and Harry continued. "Malvine told us that when he made that turn, the boat listed dangerously to starboard, and she watched until it righted itself."

Nibber turned to Debbie. "Starboard is right," he said. "Port is left." He paused, leaning this way and that on the chaise, following the course of the boat. "Of course," he finally said. "The driver had to be left-handed." He considered his conclusion for a second. "And, he was pretty stupid as well, if you ask me. A man using a tiller to steer a small boat doesn't often make sharp turns to the inside."

Harry was anxious not to leave anything out. "Kelly told me this afternoon that yesterday the state boys went back to Mal's house and asked her to repeat her story. She told them the same things she told us, but when they pressed her, she suddenly realized that the man she saw driving the boat was on the right side of the stern, not the left, where Horatio would have been. Kelly said Mal was mighty proud to have contributed, and that she was warned a number of times to keep her mouth shut. Of course, it'll all come out in a day or so, and she'll be parading like a peacock."

Diane was truly amazed. "So, Rafferty gets nailed by the very same evidence that sets Horatio free." She shook her head. "I have to say, that attorney of yours sure did make a fast five grand. His client goes free without him doing a lick of work."

Harry said he didn't care. "Don't forget," he said, "he took care of Pond Park for us, and," he added, "a speeding ticket for Nibber."

"Well, I'll be a monkey's uncle," Nibber exclaimed, slapping Debbie's thigh instead of his own. "We've just got to be the best damn detectives ever there was."

Diane had suddenly gone quiet, and Harry thought perhaps she was preparing Rafferty's defense when she suddenly looked up and made a startling announcement. "The dam's broken," she said, wide eyed.

"How can that possibly be?" Harry asked. "No rain. No phone calls. What are you talking about?"

Diane pointed to the floor under her seat. "*My* dam," she said.

Nibber sprang to his feet. "The amniotic membranes have ruptured and the uterus contractions have begun," he announced. "Baby Primip is on the way."

Harry sat transfixed, both by Nibber's medical descriptions and the growing puddle on the floor.

Nibber promptly took charge, whacked Harry on the back of the head. "Get the hospital bag," he said, nodding toward the bundle by the door as he fished for his keys. "I'll drive."

CPSIA information can be obtained at www.ICGtesting.com
Printed in the USA
BVOW03s1541280314

349091BV00007B/59/P

9 780945 980773